William Richardson

Essays on Shakespeare's Dramatic Characters of Macbeth, Hamlet,

Jaques, and Imogen

To which are prefixed an introd

William Richardson

Essays on Shakespeare's Dramatic Characters of Macbeth, Hamlet, Jaques, and Imogen
To which are prefixed an introd

ISBN/EAN: 9783337412531

Printed in Europe, USA, Canada, Australia, Japan

Cover: Foto ©Andreas Hilbeck / pixelio.de

More available books at **www.hansebooks.com**

E S S A Y S

ON

SHAKESPEARE'S

DRAMATIC CHARACTERS

OF

MACBETH, HAMLET, JAQUES, AND IMOGEN.

TO WHICH ARE PREFIXED, AN

INTRODUCTION.

THE FOURTH EDITION.

—————————

By MR. RICHARDSON,

PROFESSOR OF HUMANITY IN THE UNIVERSITY
OF GLASGOW.

—————————

LONDON:

PRINTED FOR J. MURRAY, Nº. 32,
FLEET-STREET.

M.DCC.LXXXVI.

INSCRIBED

MOST RESPECTFULLY

TO

ROBERT BUNTINE, Esq.

OF ARDOCH,

IN TESTIMONY OF THE ESTEEM

AND GRATITUDE OF

HIS MOST OBEDIENT, AND

MOST HUMBLE SERVANT,

WILLIAM RICHARDSON.

Glasgow College,
March 7, 1774. }

E S S A Y   I.

ON THE

DRAMATIC CHARACTER

O F

KING RICHARD THE THIRD.

THE " Life and Death of King " Richard the Third " is a popular tragedy: yet the poet, in his principal character, has connected deformity of body with every vice that can pollute human nature. Nor are thofe vices difguifed or foftened. The hues and lineaments are as dark and as deeply impreffed as we are capable of conceiving. Neither do they receive any confiderable mitigation from the virtues of any other

A   perfons

perfons reprefented in the poem. The
vices of Richard are not to ferve as a foil
or a teft to *their* virtues; for the virtues
and innocence of others ferve no other
purpofe than to aggravate his hideous
guilt. In reality, we are not much at-
tached by affection, admiration, or efteem,
to any character in the tragedy. The
merit of Edward, Clarence, and fome
others, is fo undecided, and has fuch a
mixture of weaknefs, as hinders us from
entering deeply into their interefts. Richmond is fo little feen, his goodnefs is fo
general or unfeatured, and the difficulties he has to encounter are fo remote
from view, are thrown, if I may ufe the
expreffion, fo far into the back ground,
and are fo much leffened by concurring
events, that he cannot, with any propriety, be deemed the hero of the performance. Neither does the pleafure we
receive proceed entirely from the gratification of our refentment, or the due dif-

play

play of poetical juſtice. To be pleaſed with ſuch a diſplay, it is neceſſary that we enter deeply into the intereſts of thoſe that ſuffer. But ſo ſtrange is the ſtructure of this tragedy, that we are leſs intereſted in the miſeries of thoſe that are oppreſſed, than we are moved with indignation againſt the oppreſſor. The ſufferers, no doubt, excite ſome degree of compaſſion; but, as we have now obſerved, they have ſo little claim to eſteem, are ſo numerous and diſunited, that no particular intereſt of this ſort takes hold of us during the whole exhibition. Thus, were the pleaſure we receive to depend ſolely on the fulfilment of poetical juſtice, that half of it would be loſt which ariſes from great regard for the ſufferers, and eſteem for the hero who performed the exploit. We may alſo add, that if the puniſhment of Richard were to conſtitute our chief enjoyment, that event is put off for too long a period. The poet might

have

have exhibited his cruelties in shorter space, sufficient, however, to excite our resentment; and so might have brought us sooner to the catastrophe, if that alone was to have yielded us pleasure. In truth, the catastrophe of a good tragedy is only the completion of our pleasure, and not the chief cause of it. The fable, and the view which the poet exhibits of human nature, conducted through a whole performance, must produce our enjoyment. But in the work now before us there is scarcely any fable; and there is no character of eminent importance, but that of Richard. He is the principal agent; and the whole tragedy is an exhibition of guilt, where abhorrence for the criminal is much stronger than our interest in the sufferers, or esteem for those, who, by accident rather than great exertion, promote his downfal. We are pleased, no doubt, with his punishment; but the display of his enormities, and their progress

to

to this completion, are the chief objects of our attention. Thus Shakefpeare, in order to render the fhocking vices of Richard an amufing fpectacle, muft have recourfe to other expedients than thofe ufually practifed in fimilar fituations. Here, then, we are led to enquire into the nature of thefe refources and expedients : for why do we not turn from the Richard of Shakefpeare, as we turn from his Titus Andronicus? Has he invefted him with any charm, or fecured him by fome fecret talifman from difguft and averfion? The fubject is curious, and deferves our attention.

Here, then, we may obferve in general, that the appearance is produced, not by veiling or contrafting offenfive features and colours, but by fo connecting them with agreeable qualities refiding in the character itfelf, that the difagreeable effect is either entirely fuppreffed, or by its unio with coalefcing qualities, is con-

verted

verted into a pleafurable feeling *. In particular, though Richard has no fenfe of juftice, nor indeed of any moral obligation, he has an abundant fhare of thofe qualities which are termed intellectual. Deftitute of virtue, he poffeffes ability. He fhews difcernment of character; artful contrivance in forming projects; great addrefs in the management of mankind; fertility of refource; a prudent command of temper; much verfatility of deportment; and fingular dexterity in concealing his intentions. He poffeffes along with thefe, fuch perfect confcioufnefs of the fuperior powers of his own underftanding, above thofe of other men, as leads him not oftentatioufly to treat them with contempt, but to employ them, while he really contemns their weaknefs, as engines of his ambition. Now, though thefe properties are not the objects of moral

---

* See Hume's Effay on Tragedy.

moral approbation, and may be employed as the inftruments of fraud no lefs than of juftice, yet the native and unmingled effect which *moft* of them produce on the fpectator, independent of the principle that employs them, is an emotion of plea-fure. The perfon poffeffing them is re-garded with deference, with refpect, and with admiration. Thus, then, the fatis-faction we receive in contemplating the character of Richard, in the various fitua-tions in which the poet has fhewn him, arifes from a mixed feeling; a feeling, compounded of horror, on account of his guilt; and of admiration, on account of his talents. By the concurrence of thefe two emotions the mind is thrown into a ftate of unufual agitation; neither painful nor pleafant, in the extremes of pain or of pleafure, but ftrangely * delightful. Surprife and amazement, excited by the

A 4   ftriking

---

* Lætatur turbidum. Hor.

ftriking conjunctures which he himfelf
very often occafions, and which give exercife to his talents, together with aftonifhment at the determined boldnefs and fuccefs of his guilt, give uncommon force to
the general impreffion.

It may be apprehended, that the mixed
feelings now mentioned may be termed indignation; nor have I any objection to the
ufe of the term. Indignation feems to
arife from a comparative view of two objects; the one worthy, and the other unworthy; which are, neverthelefs, united;
but which, on account of the wrong or
impropriety occafioned by this incongruous union, we conceive fhould be difunited and independent. The man of
merit fuffering neglect or contempt, and
the unworthy man raifed to diftinction,
provoke indignation. In like manner,
indignation may be provoked, by feeing
illuftrious talents perverted to inhuman
and perfidious purpofes. Nor is the feeling,
for

for it arifes from elevation of foul and confcioufnefs of virtue, by any means difagreeable. Indeed, the pleafure it yields us is different from that arifing from other emotions of a more placid and fofter character; different, for example, in a very remarkable manner, from our fympathy with fuccefsful merit. We may alfo obferve, that fufpence, wonder, and furprife, occafioned by the actual operation of great abilities, under the guidance of uncontrouled inhumanity, by their awful effects, and the poftures they affume, together with anxiety to fee an union fo unworthy diffolved, give poignancy to our indignation, and annex to it, if I may ufe the expreffion, a certain wild and alarming delight.

But, by what term foever we recognife the feeling, I proceed to illuftrate, by a particular analyfis of fome ftriking fcenes in the tragedy, " that the pleafure we re-"ceive from the Character of Richard,

" is

" is produced by thofe emotions which
" arife in the mind, on beholding great
" intellectual ability employed for inhu-
" man and perfidious purpofes."

I. In the firft fcene of the tragedy we
have the loathfome deformity of Richard
difplayed, with fuch indications of mind as
altogether fupprefs our averfion. Indeed
the poet, in the beginning of Richard's
foliloquy, keeps that deformity to which
he would reconcile us, out of view; nor
mentions it till he throws difcredit upon
its oppofite : this he does indirectly. He
poffeffes the imagination with diflike at
thofe employments which are the ufual
concomitants of grace and beauty. The
means ufed for this purpofe are fuited to
the artifice of the defign. Richard does
not inveigh with grave and with folemn
declamation againft the fports and paftime
of a peaceful Court : they are unworthy
of fuch ferious affault. He treats them
with irony : he fcoffs at them; does not
blame, but defpife them.

Now are our brows bound with victorious wreaths;
Our bruifed arms hung up for monuments;
Our ftern alarms changed to merry meetings;
Our dreadful marches to delightful meafures.
Grim-vifaged war hath fmooth'd his wrinkled front;
And now, inftead of mounting barbed fteeds,
To fright the fouls of fearful adverfaries,
He capers nimbly in a lady's chamber,
To the lafcivious pleafing of a lute.

By thus throwing difcredit on the ufual attendants of grace and beauty, he leffens our efteem for thofe qualities; and proceeds with lefs reluctance to mention his own hideous appearance. Here, too, with great judgment on the part of the poet, the fpeech is ironical. To have juftified or apologized for deformity with ferious argument, would have been no lefs ineffectual than a ferious charge againft beauty. The intention of Shakefpeare is not to make us admire the monftrous deformity of Richard, but to make us endure it.

But I that am not fhap'd for fportive tricks,
Nor made to court an am'rous looking-glafs;

I that

I that am rudely ſtampt, and want Love's majeſty
To ſtrut before a wanton ambling nymph;
I that am curtail'd of this fair proportion,
Cheated of feature by diſſembling nature,
Deform'd, unfiniſh'd, ſent before my time
Into this breathing world; ſcarce half made up,
And that ſo lamely and unfaſhionably,
That dogs bark at me as I halt by them:
Why I (in this weak piping time of peace)
Have no delight to paſs away the time,
Unleſs to ſee my ſhadow in the ſun,
And deſcant on mine own deformity:
And, therefore, ſince I cannot prove a lover,
To entertain theſe fair well-ſpoken days,
I am determined to prove a villain,
And hate the idle pleaſures of theſe days.

His contempt of external appearance,
and the eaſy manner in which he con-
ſiders his own defects, impreſs us ſtrongly
with the apprehenſion of his ſuperior underſtanding. His reſolution, too, of not
acquieſcing tamely in the misfortune of
his form, but of making it a motive for
him to exert his other abilities, gives us
an idea of his poſſeſſing great vigour and
ſtrength of mind. Not diſpirited with

his

his deformity, it moves him to high exertion. Add to this, that our wonder and
aftonifhment are excited at the declaration he makes of an atrocious character;
of his total infenfibility; and refolution to
perpetrate the blackeft crimes.

> Plots have I laid, inductions dangerous,
> By drunken prophecies, libels and dreams,
> To fet my brother Clarence and the king
> In deadly hate, the one againft the other;
> And if King Edward be as true and juft,
> As I am fubtle, falfe, and treacherous,
> This day fhould Clarence clofely be mew'd up.

It may be faid, perhaps, that the colouring here is by far too ftrong, and that
we cannot fuppofe characters to exift fo
full of deliberate guilt, as thus to contemplate a criminal conduct without
fubterfuge, and without impofing upon
themfelves. It may be thought, that
even the Neros and the Domitians, who
difgraced human nature, did not confider
themfelves

themſelves ſo atrociouſly wicked as they really were; but, tranſported by lawleſs paſſions, deceived themſelves, and were barbarous without perceiving their guilt. It is difficult to aſcertain what the real ſtate of ſuch perverted characters may be; nor is it a pleaſing taſk to analyſe their conceptions *. Yet the view which Shakeſpeare has given us of Richard's ſedate and deliberate guilt, knowing that his conduct was really guilty, is not inconſiſtent. He only gives a deeper ſhade to the darkneſs of his character. With his other enormities and defects, he repreſents him incapable of feeling, though he may perceive the difference between virtue and vice. Moved by unbounded ambition; vain of his intellectual and political talents; conceiving himſelf, by reaſon of his deformity, as of a different ſpecies from the reſt of mankind; and inured

* Butler.

inured from his infancy to the barbarities
perpetrated during a defperate civil war;
furely it is not incompatible with his
character, to reprefent him incapable of
feeling thofe pleafant or unpleafant fenfations that ufually, in other men, accom-
pany the difcernment of right and of wrong.
I will indeed allow, that the effect would
have been as powerful, and the reprefentation would have been better fuited to
our ideas of human nature, had Richard,
both here and in other fcenes, given
indication of his guilt rather by obfcure
hints and furmifes, than by an open declaration.

II. In the fcene between Richard and
Lady Anne, the attempt feems as bold,
and the fituation as difficult, as any in the
tragedy.

It feems, indeed, altogether wild and
unnatural, that Richard, deformed and
hideous as the poet reprefents him, fhould
offer himfelf a fuitor to the widow of an

excellent

excellent young prince whom he had flain, at the very time fhe is attending the funeral of her hufband, and while fhe is expreffing the moft bitter hatred againft the author of her misfortune. But, in attending to the progrefs of the dialogue, we fhall find ourfelves more interefted in the event, and more aftonifhed at the boldnefs and ability of Richard, than moved with abhorrence at his fhamelefs effrontery, or offended with the improbability of the fituation.

In confidering this fcene, it is neceffary that we keep in view the character of Lady Anne. The outlines of this character are given us in her own converfation; but we fee it more completely finifhed and filled up, indirectly indeed, but not lefs diftinctly, in the conduct of Richard. She is reprefented by the poet, of a mind altogether frivolous; incapable of deep affection; guided by no fteady principles of virtue, produced or ftrength-

cned

ened by reafon and reflection; the prey of vanity, which is her ruling paffion; fufceptible of every feeling and emotion; fincere in their expreffion while they laft; but hardly capable of diftinguifhing the propriety of one more than another; and fo expofed alike to the influence of good and of bad impreffions. There are fuch characters: perfons of great fenfibility, of great fincerity, of no rational or fteady virtue, and confequently of no confiftency of conduct. They now amaze us with their amiable virtues; and now confound us with apparent vices.

Richard, in his management of Lady Anne, having in view the accomplifhment of his ambitious defigns, addreffes her with the moft perfect knowledge of her conftitution. He knows that her feelings are violent; that they have no foundation in fteady determined principles of conduct; that violent feelings are foon exhaufted; and that the undecided mind,

B   without

without choice or fenfe of propriety, is equally acceffible to the next that occur. All that he has to do, then, is to fuffer the violence of one emotion to, pafs away, and then, as fkilfully as poffible, to bring another, more fuited to his defigns, into its place. Thus he not only difcovers much difcernment of human nature, but alfo great command of temper, and great dexterity of conduct.

In order, as foon as poffible, to exhauft her temporary grief and refentment, it is ne-ceffary that they be fwollen and exafperated to their utmoft meafure. In truth, it is refentment, rather than grief, which fhe expreffes in her lamentation for Henry. Accordingly Richard, inflaming her dif-order to its fierceft extreme, breaks in abruptly upon the funeral proceffion. This ftimulates her refentment; it becomes more violent, by his appearing altogether cool and unconcerned at her abufe; and

2   thus

thus she vents her emotion in fierce invectives and imprecations :

O God, which this blood mad'st, revenge his death!
O earth, which this blood drink'st, revenge his death!
Or heav'n, with light'ning strike the murderer dead!
Or earth, gape open wide, and eat him quick!

This invective is general. But before the vehemence of this angry mood can be entirely abated, she must bring home to her fancy every aggravating circumstance, and must ascertain every particular wrong she has suffered. When she has done this, and expressed the consequent feelings, she has no longer any topics or food for anger, and the passion will of course subside. Richard, for this purpose, pretends to justify or to extenuate his seeming offences; and thus, instead of concealing his crimes, he overcomes the resentment of Lady Anne, by bringing his cruelties into view. This has also the effect of impressing her with the belief of his candour.

Vouchsafe,

·Vouchfafe, divine perfection of a woman,
Of thefe fuppofed crimes, to give me leave,
By circumftance but to acquit myfelf, &c.

    ANNE. Didft thou not kill this king?

    GLO. I grant ye.

    ANNE. Doft thou grant me? then God grant me, too,
Thou may'ft be damned for that wicked deed.

Here alfo we may obferve the application of thofe flatteries and apparent ob-
fequioufnefs, which, if they cannot take
effect at prefent, otherwife than to give
higher provocation, yet, when her wrath
fubfides, will operate in a different direction, and tend to excite that vanity which
is the predominant difpofition of her mind,
and by means of which he will accomplifh
his purpofe.

It was not alone fufficient to provoke
her anger and her refentment to the utmoft, in order that they might immediately fubfide; but by alledging apparent
reafons for change of fentiment, to affift
them in their decline. Though Lady
Anne poffeffes no decided, determined
virtue,

virtue, yet her moral nature, unculti-
vated as it appears, would difcern impropriety in her conduct; would fuggeft
fcruples, and fo produce hefitation. Now,
in order to prevent the effect of thefe, it
was neceffary to aid the mind in finding
fubterfuge or excufe, and thus affift her
in the pleafing bufinefs of impofing upon
herfelf. Her feducer accordingly endeavours to glofs his conduct, and reprefents
himfelf as lefs criminal than fhe at firft
apprehended.

To leave this keen encounter of our wits,
And fall fomething into a flower method :
Is not the caufer of the timelefs deaths
Of thefe Plantagenets, Henry and Edward,
As blameful as the executioner?
 ANNE. Thou waft the caufe, and moft accurft
  effect.
 GLO. Your beauty was the caufe of that effect:
Your beauty, that did haunt me in my fleep, &c.

In thefe lines, befides a confirmation
of the foregoing remark, and an illuftra-

      tion

tion of Richard's perfevering flattery, there
are two circumftances that mark great
delicacy and finenefs of pencil in Shakefpeare's execution of this ftriking fcene.
The invective and refentment are now fo
mitigated and brought down, that the converfation, affuming the more patient form
of dialogue, is not fo much the expreffion
of violent paffion, as a conteft for victory
in a fmart difpute, and becomes a " keen
" encounter of wits." The other circumftance to be obferved is, that Richard,
inftead of fpeaking of her hufband and
father-in-law, in the relation in which
they ftood to her, falls in with the fubfiding
ftate of her affection towards them, and
ufing terms of great indifference, fpeaks
of " thefe Plantagenets, Henry and Ed-
" ward."

Lady Anne having liftened to the converfation of Richard, after the firft tranfport of her wrath on the fubject of Edward's death, fhewed that the real force

of

of the paffion was abating; and it feems to be perfectly fubdued, by her having liftened to his exculpation. In all this, the art of the poet is wonderful; and the fkill he afcribes to Richard, profound. Though the crafty feducer attempts to juftify his conduct to Lady Anne, he does not feek to convince her reafon; for fhe had no reafon worth the pains of convincing; but to afford her fome means and opportunity to vent her emotion. When this effect is produced, he proceeds to fubftitute fome regard for himfelf in its place. As we have already obferved, he has been taking meafures for this purpofe in every thing he has faid; and by foothing expreffions of adulation during the courfe of her anger, he was gradually preparing her mind for the more pleafing, but not lefs powerful, dominion of vanity. In the foregoing lines, and in what follows, he ventures a declaration of the paffion he entertains for her. Yet he

docs

does this indirectly, as fuggefted by the tendency of their argument, and as a reafon for .thofe parts of his conduct that feem fo heinous:

Your beauty was the caufe, &c.

Richard was well aware, that a declaration of love from him would of courfe renew her indignation. He accordingly manages her mind in fuch a manner as to foften its violence, by fuggefting the idea of his paffion, in the part of the dialogue containing, in his language, the " keen encounter of their wits," as a matter not altogether ferious ; and afterwards when he announces it more ferioufly, by mentioning it as it were by chance, and indirectly. Still, however, with thofe precautions to introduce the thought with an eafy and familiar appearance, it muft excite violent indignation. Here, therefore, as in the former part of the fcene, he muft have recourfe to the

fame

fame command of temper, and to the fame means of artfully irritating her emotion, till it entirely fubfides. Accordingly, he adheres without deviation to his plan; he perfifts in his adulation; provokes her anger to its utmoft excefs; and finally, by varying the attitudes of his flatteries; by affuming an humble and fuppliant addrefs, he fubdues and reftores her foul to the ruling paffion. In the clofe of the dialogue, the decline of. her emotion appears diftinctly traced. It follows the fame courfe as the paffion fhe expreffes in the beginning of the fcene. She is at firft violent; becomes more violent; her paffion fubfides; yet, fome ideas of propriety wandering acrofs her mind, fhe makes an effort to recal her refentment. The effort is feeble; it only enables her to exprefs contempt in her afpect; and at laft fhe becomes the prey of her vanity. In the concluding part of the dialogue, fhe does not, indeed, directly

comply

comply with the fuit of Richard, but indicates plainly that total change in her difpofition which it was his purpofe to produce.

III. We fhall now confider the manner in which Richard manages his accomplices, and thofe from whom he derives his affiftance in the fulfilment of his defigns.

We difcern in his conduct towards them, as much at leaft as in their own deportment, the true colour of their characters: we difcern the full extent of their faculties, and the real value of their virtues. According as they are varioufly conftituted, his treatment of them varies. He ufes them all as the tools of his ambition; but affumes an appearance of greater friendfhip and confidence towards fome than towards others. He is well acquainted with the engines he would employ: he knows the compafs of their powers, and difcovers great dexterity in

his

his manner of moving and applying them.
To the Mayor and his followers he affects
an appearance of uncommon devotion and
piety ; great zeal for the public welfare ;
a fcrupulous regard for the forms of law
and of juftice ; retirement from the world ;
averfion to the toils of ftate ; much truft
in the good intentions of a magiftrate fo
confpicuous ; ftill more in his underftanding ; and by means of both, perfect confidence in his power with the people.—
Now, in this manner of conducting himfelf, who is not more ftruck with the addrefs and ability difplayed by Richard,
and more moved with curiofity to know
their effects, than fhocked at his hypo-
crify and bafe deceit ? Who does not diftinctly, though indirectly, indeed, difcern
the character of the Mayor ? The deportment of Richard is a glafs that reflects
every limb, every lineament, and every
colour, with the moft perfect truth and
propriety.

·What,

What, think you we are Turks or Infidels,
Or that we would, againſt the form of law,
Proceed thus raſhly in the villain's death ? &c,

Alas ! why would you heap thoſe cares on me ?
I am unfit for State or Majeſty, &c.

The behaviour of Richard towards Buckingham is ſtill more ſtriking and pe-- culiar. The ſituation was more difficult, and his conduct appears more maſterly. Yet, as in former inſtances, the outlines and ſketch of Buckingham's character are filled up in the deportment of his ſe- ducer.

This accomplice poſſeſſes ſome talents, and conſiderable diſcernment of human nature : his paſſions are ardent ; he has little zeal for the public welfare, or the intereſts of virtue or religion ; yet, to a certain degree, he poſſeſſes humanity and a ſenſe of duty. He is moved with the love of power and of wealth. He is ſuſceptible, perhaps, of envy againſt thoſe who

who arife to fuch pre-eminence as he thinks might have fuited his own talents and condition. Poffeffing fome political abilities, or at leaft poffeffing that cunning, that power of fubtile contrivance, and that habit of activity, which fometimes pafs for political abilities, and which, impofing upon thofe who poffefs them, make them fancy themfelves endowed with the powers of diftinguifhed ftatefmen; he values himfelf for his talents, and is defirous of difplaying them. Indeed, this feems to be the moft ftriking feature in his character; and the defire of exhibiting his fkill and dexterity, appears to be the foremoft of his active principles. Such a perfon is Buckingham; and the conduct of Richard is perfectly confonant. Having too much penetration, or too little regard to the public weal, to be blindfolded or impofed upon like the Mayor, Richard treats him with apparent confidence. Moved, per-

haps,

haps, with envy againſt the kindred of the Queen, or the hope of pre-eminence in conſequence of their ruin, he concurs in the accompliſhment of their deſtruction, and in aſſiſting the Uſurper to attain his unlawful preferment. But above all, exceſſively vain of his talents, Richard borrows aid from his counſels, and not only uſes him as the tool of his deſigns, but ſeems to ſhare with him in the glory of their ſucceſs. Knowing, too, that his ſenſe of virtue is faint, or of little power, and that the ſecret exultation and triumph for over-reaching their adverſaries, will afford him pleaſure ſufficient to counter-balance the pain that may ariſe in his breaſt from the perpetration of guilt, he makes him, in a certain degree, the confident of his crimes. It is alſo to be remarked, that Buckingham, elated with the hope of reward, and elated ſtill more with vanity in the diſplay of his talents, appears more active than the Uſurper himſelf;

himfelf; more inventive in the contrivance of expedients, and more alert in their execution. There are many fuch perfons, the inftruments of defigning men: perfons of fome ability, of lefs virtue, who derive confequence to themfelves, by fancying they are privy to the vices or defigns of men whom they refpect, and who are lifted with triumph in the fulfilment of crafty projects. Richard, however, fees the flightnefs of Buckingham's mind, and reveals no more of his projects and vices than he reckons expedient for the accomplifhment of his purpofe: for, as fome men, when at variance, fo reftrain their refentments as to leave room for future reconciliation and friendfhip; fo Richard manages his feeming friendfhips, as to leave room, without the hazard of material injury to himfelf, for future hatred and animofity. A rupture of courfe enfues, and in a manner perfectly compatible with both of their characters.

Richard

Richard wifhes for the death of his brother Edward's children; and that his friend fhould on this, as on former occafions, partake of the fhame or the glory. But here the ambition or envy of Buckingham had no particular concern; nor was there any great ability requifite for the affaffination of two deftitute infants. Thus his humanity and fenfe of duty, feeble as they were, when expofed to ftronger principles, not altogether extinguifhed, were left to work uncontrouled; and confequently would fuggeft hefitation. They might be aided in their operation by the infatiate defire of reward for former fervices, not gratified according to promife or expectation; and, by the fame invidious difpofition, transferred from the ruined kindred of the Queen to the fuccefsful Ufurper. Richard, fomewhat aware that this project was more likely to encounter fcruples than any of the former, hints his defign with caution: he infinuates it with

acknow-

acknowledgment of obligation; and endeavours to anticipate his confcience, by
fuggefting to him, along with this acknowledgment, the recollection of former guilt.
Not aware, however, of the force con-
tained in the refifting principles, and apprehending that the mind of his affiftant
was now as depraved as he defired, he
hazards too abruptly the mention of his
defign. The confequence, in perfect confiftency with both their natures, is coldnefs
and irreconcileable hatred.

> RICH. Stand all apart.—Coufin of Buckingham—
> BUCK. My gracious Sovereign!
> 'RICH. Give me thy hand. Thus high, by thy advice
> And thy affiftance, is King Richard feated:
> But fhall we wear thefe glories for a day?
> Or fhall they laft, and we rejoice in them?
> BUCK. Still live they, and for ever let them laft.
> RICH. Ah, Buckingham! now do I play the touch,
> To try if thou be current gold indeed:
> Young Edward lives! think now what I would fpeak.
> BUCK. Say on, my loving Lord.
> RICH. Why, Buckingham, I fay I would be King.
> BUCK. Why, fo you are, my thrice renowned
> Liege.

C

RICH.

Rich. Ha! am I a King?—'Tis fo—but Edward
lives—

Buck. True, noble Prince.

Rich. O bitter confequence!

That Edward ftill fhould live—True, noble Prince—

Coufin, thou wert not wont to be fo dull.

Shall I be plain? I wifh the baftards dead,

And I fhall have it fuddenly perform'd.

What fay'ft thou now? Speak fuddenly—be brief.

Buck. Your Grace may do your pleafure.

Rich. Tut, tut, thou art all ice; thy kindnefs
freezes:

Say, have I thy confent that they fhall die?

Buck. Give me fome breath, fome little paufe,
dear Lord,

Before I pofitively fpeak in this:

I will refolve your Grace immediately.

Cates. The King is angry; fee, he gnaws his lip.

The conduct of Richard to Catefby is
different from his deportment towards the
Mayor or Buckingham. Regarding him as
totally unprincipled, fervile, and inhuman,
he treats him like the meaneft inftrument
of his guilt. He treats him without refpect for his character, without management of his temper, and without the leaft
.appre-

apprehenfion that he has any feelings that will fhudder at his commands.

IV. We fhall now confider the decline of Richard's profperity, and the effect of his conduct on the fall of his fortunes.

By diffimulation, perfidy, and blood-fhed, he paves his way to the throne: by the fame inhuman means he endea-vours to fecure his pre-eminence; and has added to the lift of his crimes, the affaffination of his wife and his nephews. Meanwhile he is laying a fnare for him-felf. Not Richmond, but his own enor-mous vices, proved the caufe of his ruin. The cruelties he perpetrates, excite in the minds of his men, hatred, indignation, and the defire of revenge. But fuch is the deluding nature of vice, that of this con-fequence he is little aware. Men who lofe the fenfe of virtue, transfer their own depravity to the reft of mankind, and believe that others are as little fhock-ed with their crimes as they are them-

felves.

felves. Richard having trampled upon every fentiment of juftice, had no conception of the general abhorrence that had arifen againft him. He thought refentment might belong to the fufferers, and their immediate adherents; but, having no faith in the exiftence of a difinterefted fenfe of virtue, he appears to have felt no apprehenfion left other perfons fhould be offended with his injuftice, or inclined to punifh his inhuman guilt. Add to this, that fuccefs adminifters to his boldnefs; and that he is daily more and more inured to the practice of violent outrage. Before he obtained the diadem, he proceeded with caution; he endeavoured to impofe upon mankind the belief of his fanctified manners; he treated his affociates with fuitable deference; and feemed as dexterous in his conduct, as he was barbarous in difpofition. But caution and diffimulation required an effort; the exertion was laborious; and to be

fufpended

fufpended when no longer needful. Thus rendered familiar with perfidious cruelty; flufhed with fuccefs; more elate with confidence in his own ability, than attentive to the fuggeftions of his fufpicion; and from his incapacity of feeling moral obligation, more ignorant of the general abhorrence he had incurred, than averfe to revenge; as he becomes, if poffible, more inhuman, he certainly becomes more incautious. This appears in the wanton difplay of his real character, and of thofe vices which drew upon him even the curfes of a parent.

> Dutch. Either thou'lt die by God's juft ordinance,
> Ere from this war thou turn a conqueror;
> Or I with grief and extreme age fhall perifh,
> And never look upon thy face again:
> Therefore, take with thee my moft heavy curfe,
> Which in the day of battle tire thee more
> Than all the complete armour that thou wear'ft.

His incautious behaviour after he has arifen to fupreme authority, appears very

ftriking

ftriking in his conduct to his accomplices.
Thofe whom he formerly feduced, or deceived, or flattered, he treats with indifference or difrefpect. He conceives himfelf no longer in need of their aid : he has
no occafion, as he apprehends, to affume
difguife. Men of high rank, who fhall
feem to give him advice or affiftance, and
fo by their influence with the multitude,
reconcile them to his crimes, or bear a
part of his infamy, ceafe to be reckoned
neceffary; and he has employment for
none, but the defperate affaffin, or im-
plicit menial. All this is illuftrated in
his treatment of Buckingham. Blinded
by his own barbarity, he requires his affiftance in the death of his nephews.
Buckingham, having lefs incitement than
formerly to give him countenance in his
guilt, hefitates, and feems to refufe. Richard
is offended ; does not govern his temper
as on former occafions ; expreffes his difpleafure ; refufes to ratify the promifes he
had

had given him; behaves to him, in the refufal, with fupercilious infult, and thus provokes his refentment.

Buck. My Lord, I claim the gift, my due by
    promife,
For which your honour and your faith are pawn'd;
Th' Earldom of Hereford, and the moveables,
Which you have promifed I fhall poffefs, &c.
  Rich. Thou troubleft me; I am not in the vein.
                          [Exit.
  Buck. Is it even fo?—Repays he my deep fervice
With fuch contempt?—Made I him king for this?
O, let me think on Haftings, and be gone
To Brecknock, while my fearful head is on.

Thus the conduct of Richard involves him in danger. The minds of men are alienated from his interefts. Thofe of his former affociates, who were in public efteem, are difmiffed with indignity, and incenfed to refentment. Even fuch of his adherents as are interefted in his fortunes, on their own account, regard him with utter averfion. A ftroke aimed at him in this perilous fituation, muft prove

effectual.

effectual. He arrives at the brink of ruin, and the flighteft impulfe will pufh him down. He refembles the misfhapen rock defcribed in a fairy tale. " This afto- " nifhing rock," fays the whimfical no- velift, " was endowed, by infernal for- " cery, with the power of impetuous mo- " tion. It rolled through a flourifhing " kingdom; it crufhed down its oppo- " nents; it laid the land defolate; and " was followed by a ftream of blood. It " arrived unwittingly at an awful preci- " pice; it had no power of returning; " for the bloody ftream that purfued it " was fo ftrong, that it never rolled " back. It was pufhed from the preci- " pice; was fhivered into fragments; " and the roar of its downfal arofe unto " heaven."

The pleafure we receive from the ruin of Richard, though intimately connected with that arifing from the various difplays of his character, is, neverthelefs, diffe- rent.

:rent. We are not amazed, as formerly, :with his talents and his addrefs: but fhocked at his cruelty, our abhorrence is foftened, or converted into an agreeable feeling, by the fatisfaction we receive from his punifhment. Befides, it is a punifhment inflicted, not by the agency of an external caufe, but incurred by the natural progrefs of his vices. We are more gratified in feeing him racked with fufpicion before the battle of Bofworth; liftening from tent to tent, left his foldiers fhould meditate treafon; overwhelmed on the eve of the battle with prefages of calamity, arifing from inaufpicious remembrance; and driven, by the dread of danger, to contemplate and be fhocked at his own heinous tranfgreffions: we are more affected, and more gratified with thefe, than with the death he fo deferv- edly fuffers. Richard and his confcience had long been ftrangers. That importu- nate monitor had been difmiffed, at a very

early

early period, from his service; nor had given him the least interruption in the career of his vices. Yet they were not entirely parted. Conscience was to visit him before he died, and chose for the hour of her visitation, the eve of his death. She comes introduced by Danger; spreads before him, in hues of infernal impression, the picture of his enormities; shakes him with deep dismay; pierces his soul with a poisoned arrow; unnerves and forsakes him.

O coward Conscience, how dost thou afflict me!
The light burns blue—is it not dead midnight?
Cold, fearful drops, stand on my trembling flesh:
What! do I fear myself? There's none else by.—
Is there a murth'rer here? No:—Yes—I am.
My Conscience hath a thousand several tongues,
And ev'ry tongue brings in a several tale,
And ev'ry tale condemns me for a villain.

Upon the whole, certain objects, whether they actually operate on our senses, or be presented to the mind by imitation,
are

are difagreeable. Yet many difagreeable objects may be fo imitated, by having their deformities veiled, or by having any agreeable qualities they may poffefs, improved or brought forward, in fuch a manner, that, fo far from continuing offenfive, they afford us pleafure. Many actions of mankind are in their own nature horrible and difgufting. Mere deceit, mere grovelling appetite, cruelty and meannefs, both in the imitation and the original, occafion pain and averfion. Yet thefe vices may be fo reprefented by the fkill of an ingenious artift, as to afford us pleafure. The moft ufual method of rendering their reprefentation agreeable is, by fetting the characters in whom they predominate, in oppofition to fuch characters as are eminent for their oppofite virtues. The diffimulation, ingratitude, and inhumanity of Goneril, fet in oppofition to the native fimplicity, the filial affection, and fenfibility of Cordelia, though

in

7

in themfelves hateful, become an interefting fpectacle. The pleafure we receive is, by having the agreeable feelings and fentiments that virtue excites,
improved and rendered exquifite by contraft, by alternate hopes and fears, and
even by our fubdued and coinciding abhorrence of vice. For the painful feeling, overcome by delightful emotions,
lofes its direction and peculiar character;
but retaining its force, communicates additional energy to the prevailing fenfa-
tion, and fo augments its efficacy. Another more difficult, though no lefs interefting method of producing the fame effect
is, when, with fcarce any attention to oppofite virtues in other perfons, very ag-
gravated and heinous vices are blended
and united in the fame perfon, with agreeable intellectual qualities. Boldnefs, command of temper, a fpirit of enterprife,
united with the intellectual endowments
of difcernment, penetration, dexterity, and
addrefs,

addrefs, give us pleafure. Yet thefe may be employed as inftruments of cruelty and oppreffion, no lefs than of juftice and humanity. When the reprefentation is fuch, that the pleafure arifing from thefe qualities is ftronger than the painful averfion and abhorrence excited by concomitant vices, the general effect is agreeable. Even the painful emotion, as in the former cafe, lofing its character, but retaining its vigour, imparts additional force to our agreeable feelings. Thus, though there is no approbation of the vicious character, we are, neverthelefs, pleafed with the reprefentation. The foul is overfhadowed with an agreeable gloom, and her powers are fufpended with delightful horror. The pleafure is varied and increafed, when the criminal propenfities, gaining ftrength by indulgence, occafion the neglect of intellectual endowments, and difregard of their affiftance; fo that by natural confequence, and without the

interpofition

interpofition of uncommon agency from without, the vicious perfon, becoming as incautious as he is wicked, is rendered the prey of his own corruptions; fofters thofe fnakes in his bofom that fhall devour his vitals; and fuffers the moft condign of all punifhment, the miferies intailed by guilt.

Shakefpeare, in his Richard the Third, has chofen that his principal character fhould be conftructed according to the laft of thefe methods; and this I have endeavoured to illuftrate, by confidering the manner in which Richard is affected by the confcioufnefs of his own deformity; by confidering the dexterity of his conduct in feducing the Lady Anne; by obferving his various deportment towards his feeming friends or accomplices; and finally, by tracing the progrefs of his vices to his downfal and utter ruin.

The other excellencies of this tragedy, befides the character of Richard, are, indeed,

'deed, of an inferior nature, but not unworthy of Shakefpeare. The characters
of Buckingham, Anne, Haftings, and
Queen Margaret, are executed with lively
colouring and ftriking features; but,
excepting Margaret, they are exhibited
indirectly; and are more fully known by
the conduct of Richard towards them,
than by their own demeanour. They
give the fketch and outlines in their own
actions; but the picture appears finifhed
in the deportment of Richard. This,
however, of itfelf, is a proof of very fingular fkill. The conduct of the ftory is
not inferior to that in Shakefpeare's other
hiftorical tragedies. It exhibits a natural
progrefs of events, terminated by one interefting and complete cataftrophe. Many
of the epifodes have uncommon excellence. Of this kind are, in general, all the
fpeeches of Margaret. Their effect is
awful; they coincide with the ftyle of
the tragedy; and by wearing the fame
gloomy

gloomy complexion, her prophecies and imprecations fuit and increafe its horror. There was never in any poem a dream fuperior to that of Clarence. It pleafes, like the prophecies of Margaret, by a folemn anticipation of future events, and by its confonance with the general tone of the tragedy. It pleafes, by being fo fimple, fo natural, and fo pathetic, that every reader feems to have felt the fame or fimilar horrors; and is inclined to fay with Brakenbury,

No wonder, Lord, that it affrighted you;
I am afraid, methinks, to hear you tell it.

This tragedy, however, like every work of Shakefpeare, has many faults; and in particular, it feems to have been too haftily written. Some incidents are introduced without any apparent reafon, or without apparent neceffity in the conduct of the performance. We are not, for inftance, fufficiently informed of the motive

that

that prompted Richard to marry the widow of Prince Edward. In other respects, as was obferved, this fcene poffeffes very fingular merit. The fcene towards the clofe of the tragedy, between the Queen and Richard, when he folicits her confent to marry her daughter Elizabeth, feems no other than a copy of that now mentioned. As fuch, it is faulty; and ftill more fo, by being executed with lefs ability. Yet this incident is not liable to the objection made to the former. We fee a good, prudential reafon, for the marriage of Richard with Elizabeth; but none for his marriage with Lady Anne. We almoft wifh that the firft courtfhip had been omitted, and that the dialogue between Richard and Anne had been fuited and appropriated to Richard and the Queen. Neither are we fufficiently informed of the motives, that, on fome occafions, influenced the conduct of Buckingham. We are not enough pre-

D   pared

pared for his animofity againft the Queen and her kindred; nor can we pronounce, without hazarding conjecture, that it proceeded from envy of their fudden greatnefs, or from having his vanity flattered by the feeming deference of Richard. Yet thefe motives feem highly probable. The young Princes bear too great a fhare in the drama. It would feem the poet intended to intereft us very much in their misfortunes. The reprefentation, however, is not agreeable. The Princes have more fmartnefs than fimplicity; and we are more affected with Tyrrel's defcription of their death, than pleafed with any thing in their own converfation. Nor does the fcene of the ghofts, in the laft act, feem equal in execution to the defign of Shakefpeare. There is more delightful horror in the fpeech of Richard awakening from his dream, than in any of the predictions denounced againft him. There feems, indeed, fome impropriety

in

in reprefenting thofe fpectres as actually appearing, which were only feen in a vifion. Befides, Richard might have defcribed them in the fucceeding fcene, to Ratcliff, fo as to have produced, at leaft in the perufal of the work, a much ftronger effect. The reprefentation of ghofts in this paffage, is by no means fo affecting, nor fo awful, as the dream related by Clarence. Laftly, there is in this performance, too much deviation in the dialogue from the dignity of the bufkin ; and deviations ftill more blameable, from the language of decent manners. Yet, with thefe imperfections, this tragedy is a ftriking monument of human genius ; and the fuccefs of the poet, in delineating the character of Richard, has been as great as the fingular boldnefs of the defign.

ESSAY

DISINTERESTED principles are of different kinds: of confequence, the actions that flow from them are more or lefs beneficial, and more or lefs entitled to praife. We are moved by inconfiderate impulfe to the performance of beneficent actions; as we are moved by inconfiderate impulfe to the perpetration of guilt. You fee an unhappy perfon; you difcern the vifitation of grief in his features; you hear them in the plaintive tones of voice; you are

D 3 warmed

warmed with fudden and refiftlefs emo‐‐
tion ; you never enquire concerning the
propriety of your feelings, or the merits
of the fufferer ; and you haften to relieve
him. Your conduct proceeds from incon‐
fiderate impulfe. It entitles you to the
praife of fenfibility, but not of reflection.
You are again in the fame fituation ; but
the fymptoms of diftrefs do not produce
in you the fame ardent effects : you are
moved with no violent agitation, and you
feel little fympathy ; but you perceive
diftrefs ; you are convinced that the fuf‐
ferer fuffers unjuftly; you know you are
bound to relieve him ; and in confequence
of thefe convictions, you offer him relief.
Your conduct proceeds from fenfe of duty ;
and though it entitles you to the credit of
rational humanity, it does not entitle you,
in this inftance, to the praife of fine fen‐
fibility.

Thofe who perform beneficent actions,
from immediate feeling or impetuous im‐
pulfe,

pulfe, have a great deal of pleafure.—
Their conduct, too, by the influence of
fympathetic affection, imparts pleafure
to the beholder. The joy felt both by
the agent and the beholder is ardent, and
approaches to rapture. There is alfo an
energy in the principle, which produces
great and uncommon exertions; yet both
the principle of action, and the pleafure it
produces, are fhifting. " Beauteous as
" the morning cloud or the early dew ;"
like them, too, they pafs away. The pleafure arifing from knowledge of duty is
lefs impetuous : it has no approaches to
rapture ; it feldom makes the heart throb,
or the tear defcend ; and as it produces no
tranfporting enjoyment, it feldom leads
to uncommon exertion ; but the joy it
affords is uniform, fteady, and lafting.
As the conduct is moft perfect, fo our
happinefs is moft complete, when both
principles are united : when our convictions of duty are animated with fenfibility ;

and

and fenfibility guided by convictions of duty.

It is, indeed, to be regretted, that feeling and the knowledge of duty are not always united. It is deeply to be regretted, that unlefs fenfibility be regulated by that knowledge of duty which arifes from reflection on our own condition, and acquaintance with human nature, it may produce unhappinefs both to ourfelves and others; but chiefly to ourfelves. To illuftrate thefe confequences may be of fervice. It is often no lefs important to point out the nature and evil effects of feeming excellence, than of acknowledged depravity; befides, it will exhibit the human mind in a ftriking fituation.

The fubject, perhaps, is unpopular.— It is the fafhion of the times to celebrate feeling; and the conduct flowing from fedater principles is pronounced cold or ungenial. It is the conduct, we are told, of thofe difpaffionate minds who never deviate
ate

ate to the right hand or the left; who travel
through life unnoticed: and as they are
never vifited by the extacies of fenfibility,
they enjoy unenvied immunity from its
delicate forrows. What pretenfions have
they to the diftinction of weak nerves or
exquifite feeling? They know fo little
of the melancholy and of the refined impatience fo often the portion of fentimen-
tal fpirits, that they are abfurd enough to
term them chagrin and ill-humour. In
truth, fentiment and fenfibility have been
the fubject of fo many tales and fermons,
that the writer who would propofe the
union of feeling with reflection, may,
perhaps, incur much faftidious difdain:
we fhall, therefore, go forth upon this
adventure under the banner of a powerful and refpectable leader. Shakefpeare
was nolefs intimately acquainted with the
principles of human conduct, than excellent in delineation; and has exhibited in
his Dramatic Character of King Lear the
man of mere fenfibility.

I. Thofe

I. Thofe who are guided in their con-duct by impetuous impulfe, arifing from fenfibility, and undirected by reflection, are liable to extravagant or outrageous excefs. Tranfported by their own emotions, they mifapprehend the condition of others : they are prone to exaggeration ; and even the good actions they perform, excite amazement rather than approbation. Lear, an utter ftranger to adverfe fortune, and under the power of exceffive affection, conceived his children in every refpect deferving. During this ardent and inconfiderate mood, he afcribed to them fuch correfponding fentiments as juftified his extravagant fondnefs. He faw his children as the gentleft and moft affectionate of the human race. What con-defcenfion, on his part, could be a fuitable reward for their filial piety ? He divides his kingdom among them ; they will relieve him from the cares of royalty ; and to his old age will afford confolation.

H:

He fhakes all cares and bufinefs from his age,
Conferring them on younger ftrengths.

But he is not only extravagant in his
love; he is no lefs outrageous in his difpleafure.   Kent, moved with zeal for his
intereft, remonftrates, with the freedom
of confcious integrity, againft his conduct to Cordelia; and Lear, impatient of
good counfel, not only rebukes him with
unbecoming afperity, but inflicts unme-
rited punifhment.

Five days we do allot thee for previfion,
To fhield thee from difafters of the world ;
And on the fixth to turn thy hated back
Upon our kingdom: if on the tenth day following
Thy banifh'd trunk be found in our dominions,
The moment is thy death.

II. The conduct proceeding from unguid-
ed feeling will be *capricious*. In minds where
principles of regular and permanent influence have no authority, every feeling
has a right to command ; and every impulfe, how fudden foever, is regarded,
during

during the feafon of its power, with entire approbation.

All fuch feelings and impulfes are not only admitted, but obeyed ; and lead us, without hefitation or reflection, to a corresponding deportment. But the objects with which we are converfant, often vary their afpects, and are feen by us in different attitudes. This may be owing to accidental connection or comparifon with other things, of a fimilar or of a different nature ; or it may be owing, and this is moft frequently the cafe, to fome accidental mood or humour of our own. A fine landfcape, viewed in different lights, fhall appear more or lefs beautiful ; yet the landfcape in itfelf fhall remain unaltered ; nor will the perfon who views it pronounce it in reality lefs beautiful than it was, though he fees it with a fetting rather than with a rifing fun. The capricious inconftancy of their character is very apt to difplay itfelf, when unfortunately

nately they form expectations, and fuſ-
tain diſappointments. Moved by an ardent mood, they regard the objects of
their affection with extravagant tranſport; they transfer to them their own
diſpoſitions; they make no allowance for
differences of condition or ſtate of mind;
and expect returns ſuitable to their own
unreaſonable ardours. They are diſappointed; they feel pain: in proportion to
the violence of the diſappointed paſſion,
is the pang of repulſe. This rouſes a ſenſe
of wrong, and excites their reſentment.
The new feelings operate with as much
force as the former. No enquiry is made
concerning the reaſonableneſs of the conduct they would produce. Reſentment
and indignation are felt; and merely be-
cauſe they are felt, they are deemed juſt
and becoming.

Cordelia was the favourite daughter of
Lear. His ſiſters had replied to him,
with an extravagance ſuited to the extravagance

travagance of his affection. He expected much more from Cordelia. Yet her
reply was better fuited to the relation
that fubfifted betweeen them, than to the
fondnefs of his prefent humour. He is
difappointed, pained, and provoked. There
is no gentle advocate in his bofom to mi-
tigate the rigours of his difpleafure. He
follows the blind impulfe of his refentment ; abufes and abandons Cordelia.

Let it be fo; thy truth then be thy dower :
For, by the facred radiance of the fun,
Here I difclaim all my paternal care,
Propinquity and property of blood;
And, as a ftranger to my heart and me,
Hold thee from this for ever.

Unhappy are they who have eftablifhed
no fyftem concerning the character of
their friends ; and who have afcertained,
by the aid of reafon or obfervation, no
meafure of their virtues or infirmities.
There is no affectionate inmate in their
bofoms, the vicegerent of indulgent affection,

fection, to plead in your behalf, if from
inadvertency, or the influence of a way-
ward, but tranfient mood, affecting either
you or themfelves, you act differently
from your wonted conduct, or differently
from their expectations.   Thus their appearances are as variable as that of the
camelion : they now fhine with the faireft
colours; and in an inftant they are changed
into fable.   In vain would you afk for.
a reafon.   You may enquire of the winds;
or queftion their morning dreams.   Yet
they are ardent in proteftations ; they
give affurances of lafting attachment ;
but they are not to be trufted.   Not that
they intend to deceive you.   They have
no fuch intention.   They are veffels
without rudder or anchor, driven by
every blaft that blows.   Their affurances
are the colours impreffed by a fun-beam
on the breaft of a watery cloud : they
are formed into a beautiful figure ; they
fhine for a moment with every exquifite
                                    tint ;

tint; in a moment they vaniſh, and leave nothing but a drizly ſhower in their ſtead.

III. Thoſe who are guided by inconſiderate feeling, will often appear variable in their conduct, and of courſe irreſolute. There is no variety of feeling to which perſons of great ſenſibility are more liable, than that of great elevation or depreſſion of ſpirits. The ſudden and unaccountable tranſitions from the one to the other, are not leſs ſtriking, than the vaſt difference of which we are conſcious in the one mood or in the other. In an elevated ſtate of ſpirits, we form projects, entertain hopes, conceive ourſelves capable of high exertion, think highly of ourſelves, and in this hour of tranſport, undervalue obſtacles or oppoſition. In a moment of depreſſion, the ſcene is altered: the ſky lowrs; nature ceaſes to ſmile; or if ſhe ſmiles, it is not to us; we feel ourſelves feeble, forſaken, and

hopeleſs;

hopeless; all things, human and divine,
have confpired againft us. Having no
adequate opinion of ourfelves, or no juft
apprehenfion of the ftate of opinions concerning us, we think that no great exertion or difplay of merit is expected from
us, and of courfe we grow indifferent
about our conduct. Thus the mind, at
one inftant, afpires to heaven, is bold, en-
terprifing, difdainful, and fupercilious:
the wind changes—we are baffled or fa-
tigued; and the fpirit formerly fo full of
ardour, becomes humble and paffive.

Lear had fuffered infult and ingratitude
from his eldeft daughter. He boils with
refentment; he expreffes it with imprecations, and leaves her: but his mind,
haraffed and teazed, fuffers fore agitation,
and is enfeebled. He looks of courfe for
relief; indulges confidence in his fecond
daughter; from her he expects confolation; anticipates a kindly reception;
yields to that depreffion of mind, which
E   is

is connected with the wish and expectation of pity; he longs to complain; and to mingle his tears with the sympathetic sorrows of Regan. Thus entirely reduced, he discerns, even in Regan, symptoms of disaffection. Yet, in his present state, he will not believe them. They are forced upon his observation; and Kent, who was exiled for wishing to moderate his wrath against Cordelia, is obliged to stimulate his displeasure at Regan. Yet, in the weakness of his present depression, and longings for affectionate pity, he would repose on her tenderness, and addresses her with full confidence in her love:

No, Regan, thou shalt never have my curse.
——————— 'Tis not in thee
To bandy hasty words, to scant my sizes, &c.
——————— Thou better know'st
The offices of nature.

In the whole intercourse between Lear and Regan, we see a contest between Lear's

Lear's indignant and refentful emotions, excited by the indications of Regan's difaffection, and thofe fond expectations and defires of fympathetic tendernefs, which proceed from, and in their turn contribute to, depreffion of fpirit. Thus he condefcends to entreat and remonftrate:

I gave you all!

At length, repulfed and infulted by Regan, totally caft down and enfeebled, he forgets his determined hatred of Goneril; and in the mifery of his depreffion, irrefolute and inconfiftent, he addreffes her as his laft refource:

—————— Not being the worft,
Stands in fome need of praife: I'll go with thee;
Thy fifty yet doth double five and twenty,
And thou haft twice her love.

Here he is again, difappointed. He has no other refource. His mind, originally

E 2   of

of a keen and impetuous nature, is now
unoccupied by any tender fentiment.
Accordingly, at the clofe of this interefting fcene, we fee him forcing himfelf,
as it were, from his depreffion, and expreffing his undiminifhed refentment :

> You Heavens, give me that patience which I need ;
> You fee me here, you Gods, a poor old man,
> As full of grief as age ; wretched in both !
> If it be you that ftir thefe daughters' hearts
> Againft their father, fool me not fo much
> To bear it tamely ; touch me with noble anger :
> O let not womens' weapons, water-drops,
> Stain my man's cheeks : no, you unnatural hags,
> I will have fuch revenges on you both,
> That all the world fhall——I will do fuch things—
> What they are, yet I know not ; but they fhall be,
> The terrors of the earth. You think I'll weep—
> No, I'll not weep.
> I have full caufe of weeping ; but this heart
> Shall break into an hundred thoufand flaws,
> Or e'er I'll weep.—O Fool, I fhall go mad.

Inconfiftency of conduct, and of confequence, irrefolution, occafioned by irregular and undirected feelings, proceed
from

from other ſtates of mind than depreſſion
of ſpirits. Of this, ſome examples different from the preſent now occur to me.
They illuſtrate the general poſition, and
may therefore be mentioned.

Lorenzo de Medicis * had a lively fan-
·cy; he was a courtier—ambitious—and
had his imagination filled with ideas of
pageantry. He wiſhed to enjoy pre-eminence ; but his brother Alexander, the
reigning Prince, was an obſtacle to be
removed ; and this could only be done
by ſpoiling him of his life. The difficulty
no doubt was great ; yet, it figured leſs
to his heated imagination, than the dignity and enjoyment he had in view.
Elegant in his manners ; accompliſhed
with every pleaſing endowment ; of ſoft
and inſinuating addreſs ; he had, never-,
theleſs, no ſecret counſellor in his breaſt
to plead in behalf of juſtice.   Thus
            E 3   prompted

---

prompted, and thus unguarded, he perpetrates the death of his brother. He fees his blood ftreaming; hears him groaning in the agonies of death; beholds him convulfed in the pangs of departing life : a new fet of feelings arife; the delicate, accomplifhed courtier, who could meditate atrocious injury, cannot, without being afhamed, witnefs the bloody object; he remains motionlefs; irrefolute; appalled at the deed; and in this ftate of amazement, neither profecutes his defign, nor thinks of efcaping. Thus, without ftruggle or oppofition, he is feized and punifhed as he deferves.

Voltaire gives a fimilar account of his hero, Lewis. After defcribing in lively colours the defolation perpetrated by his authority in the Palatinate; the conflagration of cities, and the utter ruin of the inhabitants, he fubjoins, that thefe orders were iffued from Verfailles, from the midft of pleafures; and that, on a nearer view,

view, the calamities he thus occafioned would have filled him with horror. That is, Lewis, like all men of irregular fenfibility, was governed by the influences of objects operating immediately on his fenfes ; and fo according to fuch accidental mood as depended on prefent images, he was humane or inhuman. Lewis and Lorenzo, in thofe inftances, were men of feeling, but not of virtue. They were a-kin to Lady Macbeth, who advifed and determined the murder of Duncan, and who would have executed the deed herfelf; but with the dagger lifted, in act to ftrike, of fuch fenfibility, fo tender, fhe could not proceed—the old man refembled her father.

IV. The man of ungoverned fenfibility, is in danger of becoming morofe or inhuman. He entertains fanguine hopes ; he allows every feeling to reign in his breaft uncontrouled; his judgment is dazzled; and his imagination riots in rapturous dreams of enjoyment. Every

object

object of his wishes is arrayed in seducing colours, and brought immediately within his reach. He engages in the pursuit; encounters difficulties of which he was not aware; his ravishing expectations subside; he had made no provision for arduous adventure; his imagination becomes a traitor; the dangers and difficulties appear more formidable than they really are; and he abandons his undertaking. His temper is of consequence altered. No longer elated with hope, he becomes the prey of chagrin, of envy, or of resentment. Even suppose him successful; his enjoyments are not equal to his hopes. His desires were excessive, and no gratification whatever can allay the vehemence of their ardour. He is discontented, restless, and unhappy. In a word, irregular feelings, and great sensibility, produce extravagant desires; these lead to disappointment; and in minds that are undisciplined, disappoint-

ment

ment begets morofenefs and anger. Thefe difpofitions again will difplay themfelves, according to the condition or character of him who feels them. Men of feeble conftitutions, and without power over the fortunes of other men, under fuch malign influences, become fretful, invidious, and mifanthropical. Perfons of firmer ftructure, and unfortunately poffeffed of power, under fuch direction, become inhuman. Herod was a man of feeling. Witnefs his conduct to Mariamne. At one time elegant, courteous, and full of tendernefs; his fondnefs was as unbounded, as the virtues and graces of Mariamne were peerlefs. At other times, offended becaufe her expreffions of mutual affection were not as extravagant as the extravagance of his own emotions, he became fufpicious without caufe. Thus affectionate, fond, fufpicious, refentful, and powerful; in the phrenzy of irregular feeling, he put to death Mariamne.

Lear,

Lear, in the reprefentation of Shakefpeare, poffeffing great fenfibility, and
full of affection, feeks a kind of enjoyment fuited to his temper. Afcribing
the fame fenfibility and affection to his
daughters, for they muft have it, no
doubt, by hereditary right, he forms a
pleafing dream of repofing his old age
under the wings of their kindly protec-
tion. He is difappointed; he feels extreme pain and refentment; he vents his
refentment; but he has no power. Will
he then become morofe and retired? His
habits and temper will not give him
leave. Impetuous, and accuftomed to
authority, confequently of an unyielding
nature, he would wreak his wrath, if he
were able, in deeds of exceffive violence.
He would do, he knows not what. He
who could pronounce fuch imprecations
againft Goneril, as, notwithftanding her
guilt, appear fhocking and horrid, would,
in the moment of his refentment, have

put

put her to death If, without any ground of offence, he could abandon Cordelia, and caft off his favourite child, what would he not have done to the unnatural and pitilefs Regan?

Here, then, we have a curious fpectacle: a man accuftomed to bear rule, fuffering fore difappointment, and grievous wrongs; high minded, impetuous, fufceptible of extreme refentment; and incapable of yielding to morofe filence, or malignant retirement. What change can befall his fpirit? For his condition is fo altered, that his fpirit alfo muft fuffer change. What! but to have his underftanding torn up by the hurricane of paffion, to fcorn confolation, and lofe his reafon! Shakefpeare could not avoid making Lear diftracted. Other poets exhibit madnefs, becaufe they chufe it, or for the fake of variety, or to deepen the diftrefs: but Shakefpeare has exhibited the madnefs of Lear, as the natural effect of fuch fuffering on fuch a character

character. It was an event in the progrefs of Lear's mind, driven by fuch feelings, defires, and paffions as the poet
afcribes to him, as could not be avoided.

It is fometimes obferved, that there
are three kinds of madnefs difplayed in this
performance : that of Lear, that of Edgar ; and that of the Fool. The obfervation is inaccurate. The madnefs of
Edgar is entirely pretended ; and that of
the Fool has alfo more affectation than
reality. Accordingly, we find Lear for
ever dwelling upon one idea, and recon-
ciling every thing to one appearance.
The ftorms and tempefts were not his
daughters. The gleams of reafon that
fhoot athwart the darknefs of his diforder,
render the gloom more horrid. Edgar
affects to dwell upon one idea ; he is
haunted by fiends ; but he is not uniform.
The feeling he difcovers, and compaffion
for the diftreffes of Lear, breaking out
in fpite of his counterfeit, render his
speeches

ſpeeches very often pathetic. The Fool,
who has more honeſty than underſtanding,
and more underſtanding than he pretends,
becomes an intereſting character, by his
attachment to his unfortunate maſter.

V. Lear, thus extravagant, inconſiſtent,
inconſtant, capricious, variable, irreſolute,
and impetuouſly vindictive, is almoſt an
object of diſapprobation. But our poet,
with his uſual ſkill, blends the diſagree-
able qualities with ſuch circumſtances as
correct this effect, and form one delightful aſſemblage. Lear, in his good intentions, was without deceit; his violence is
not the effect of premeditated malignity;
his weakneſſes are not crimes, but often
the effects of miſruled affections. This
is not all: he is an old man; an old
king; an aged father; and the inſtru-
ments of his ſuffering are undutiful
children. He is juſtly entitled to our
compaſſion; and the incidents laſt mentioned, though they imply no merit, they
procure

procure fome refpect. Add to all this,
that he becomes more and more interesting towards the clofe of the drama; not
merely becaufe he is more and more unhappy, but becaufe he becomes really
more deferving of our efteem. His misfortunes correct his mifconduct; they
roufe reflection; and lead him to that reformation which we approve. We fee
the commencement of this reformation,
after he has been difmiffed by Goneril,
and meets with fymptoms of difaffection in Regan. He who abandoned Cordelia with impetuous outrage, and ba-
nifhed Kent for offering an apology in
her behalf; feeing his fervant grofsly mal-
treated, and his own arrival unwelcomed,
has already fuftained fome chaftifement:
he does not exprefs that ungoverned violence which his preceding conduct might
lead us to expect. He reftrains his emotion in its firft ebullition, and reafons'

con—

concerning the probable caufes of what feemed fo inaufpicious.

> LEAR. The King would fpeak with Cornwall; the
> dear father
> Would with his daughter fpeak, commands her fervice:
> Are they inform'd of this ?—My breath and blood !—
> Fiery—the fiery Duke ? Tell the hot Duke that—
> No—but not yet—may be he is not well—
> Infirmity doth ftill neglect all office,
> Whereto our health is bound : we're not ourfelves
> When nature, being opprefs'd, commands the mind
> To fuffer with the body—I'll forbear ;
> And am fallen out with my more heady will,
> To take the indifpofed and fickly fit,
> For the found man.

As his misfortunes increafe, we find him ftill more inclined to reflect on his fituation. He does not, indeed, exprefs blame of himfeif; yet he exprefies no fentiment whatever of overweaning conceit. He feems rational and modeft ; and, the application to himfelf is extremely, pathetic :

> ————————— Clof· pent up guilts,
> Rive your concealing continents, and afk

Thefe

Thefe dreadful fummoners grace.—I am a man
More finn'd againſt than finning.

Soon after, we find him actually pro-
nouncing cenſure upon himſelf. Hitherto
he had been the mere creature of ſenſibility; he now begins to reflect ; and grieves
that he had not done ſo before.

Poor naked wretches, whereſoe'er you are,
That bide the pelting of this pitileſs ſtorm !
How ſhall your houſeleſs heads, and unfed ſides,
Your loop'd and window'd raggedneſs defend you
From ſeaſons ſuch as theſe ?—O, I have ta'en
Too little care of this ! Take phyſic, pomp,
Expoſe thyſelf to feel what wretches feel,
That thou may'ſt ſhake the ſuperflux to them,
And ſhew the heavens more juſt.

At laſt, he is in a ſtate of perfect con-
trition, and expreſſes leſs reſentment
againſt Goneril and Regan, than ſelf-condemnation for his treatment of Cordelia,
and a perfect, but not extravagant ſenſe
of her affection.

KENT.   The poor diſtreſſed Lear's in town,
Who ſometimes in his better tune remembers

What

What we are come about, and by no means
Will yield to fee his daughter.
    GENT. Why, good Sir?
    KENT. A fovereign fhame fo bows him, his un-
        kindnefs,
That ftript her from his benediction, turn'd her
To foreign cafualties, gave her dear rights
To his dog-hearted daughter: thefe things fting him
So venomoufly, that burning fhame detains him
From his Cordelia.

I have thus endeavoured to fhew, that mere fenfibility, undirected by reflection, leads men to an extravagant expreffion both of focial or unfocial feelings; renders them capricioufly inconftant in their affections; variable, and of courfe irrefolute, in their conduct. Thefe things, together with the miferies entailed by fuch deportment, feem to me well illuftrated by Shakefpeare, in his Dramatic Character of King Lear.

ESSAY

E S S A Y III.

SHAKESPEARE, in his Timon of
Athens, illuſtrates the conſequences
of that inconſiderate profuſion which has
the appearance of liberality, and is ſuppoſed even by the inconſiderate perſon himſelf to proceed from a generous principle ;
but which, in reality, has its chief origin
in the love of diſtinction. Though this is
not the view uſually entertained of this
ſingular dramatic character, I perſuade my-
ſelf, if we attend to the deſign of the

poet

poet in all its parts, we fhall find, that the opinion now advanced is not without foundation.

The love of diftinction is afferted to be the ruling principle in the conduct of Timon; yet it is not affirmed, nor is it neceffary to affirm, that Timon has no goodnefs of heart. He has much goodnefs, gentlenefs, and love of fociety.— Thefe are not inconfiftent with the love of diftinction: they often refide together; and in particular, that love of diftinction which reigned in the conduct of Timon, may eafily be fhewn to have received its particular bias and direction from original goodnefs. For, without this, what could have determined him to chufe one method of making himfelf confpicuous rather than another? Why did he not feek the diftinction conferred by the difplay of a military or of a political character? Or why did he not afpire after pageantry and parade, the pomp of public buildings, and

the

the oftentation of wealth, unconnected with any kind of beneficence ?

In general, our love of fame or diftinction is directed and influenced by fome previous caft of temper, or early tendency of difpofition. Moved by powers and difpofitions leading us to one kind of exertion rather than another, we attribute fuperior excellence to fuch exertion. We transfer the fame fentiment to the rest of mankind. We fancy, that no pre-eminence can be attained but by fuch talents as we poffefs; and it requires an effort of cool reflection, before we can allow that there may be excellence in thofe things which we cannot relifh, or merit in that conduct to which we are not inclined. Guided by early or inherent predilection, men actuated by the love of diftinction, feek the idol of their defires in various fituations; in the buftle of active life, or in the fhade of retirement. Take the following examples. The fon of Olorus

F 3

was prefent, while yet a boy, at the Olym-
pic games. All Greece was affembled;
many feats of dexterity, no doubt, were
exhibited; and every honour that affembled Greece could beftow, was conferred
on the victors. Moved by a fpectacle
fo interefting and fo infpiriting, the Spar-
tan, Theban, or Athenian youth, who
were not yet of vigour fufficient to ftrive
for the wreath, longed, we may readily fuppofe, for maturer years; and became, in
their ardent imaginations, fkilful wreftlers
and charioteers. The fon of Olorus, if
we may judge by the confequence, felt
little emotion; no fympathetic longings;
and no impatience to drive a chariot.—
But hearing Herodotus, on that occafion,
reciting his hiftory, he felt other fenfations; his heart throbbed, and the tears
defcended. The venerable hiftorian obferved him weeping, and comprehending
his character, "I give thee joy," faid he
to his father, "for the happy genius of
"thy

" thy fon." Now, the fon of Olorus became an hiftorian no lefs renowned than
Herodotus : for Herodotus and Thucy-
dides are ufually named together. The
celebrated Turenne, in his early days, was
an admirer, no lefs paffionate, of Quintus
Curtius, than the fon of Olorus was of
Herodotus ; and we are told by Ramfay,
from D'Ablancourt, that when not yet
twelve years of age, he challenged an
officer who called his favourite hiftory
a romance. But this admiration was not
fo much for the graces of flowery compofition which abound in the Roman
hiftorian, as for the valiant actions of
Alexander. Thefe drew his attention,
and foon after, his imitation. Though
his breaft heaved, and his eyes fparkled, in
the perufal of favourite paffages, he was
not led to write fine defcriptions like Curtius ; but to break horfes like the fon of
Philip.

Now, fince thofe that are actuated by
the love of diftinction, are led, by early

F 4   or

or inherent predilection, to one kind of action rather than another, we have no difficulty in allowing principles of goodnefs and humanity to have reigned early, or originally, in the breaft of Timon. Nay, after lofing their authority, they continued for fome time to attend him; and refided in that breaft where they formerly reigned. They became like thofe eaftern princes, or thofe early fovereigns of a neighbouring country, who grew fo indolent and paffive, that they lay immured in their apartments, and left the management of the ftate to fome active minifter, an ambitious vizier, or mayor of the palace. Some of thefe minifters acted for a while under the banner of the fovereign's authority; but afterwards, having left him but the fhadow of power, they promoted themfelves; became fupreme and defpotic.

Here, however, we are led to enquire, how happens it that a principle inherent in the foul, and once an active principle,

becomes

becomes paffive, fuffers others to operate in its ftead; not only fo, but to perform fimilar functions, affume correfponding appearances, and, in general, to be guided apparently to the fame tenor of conduct? Did the energy of the inherent affection fuffer abatement by frequent exercife? Or were there no kindred principles in the foul to fupport and confirm its authority? Could not reafon, or the fenfe of duty, fupport, and the power of active habit confirm? How came the fultan to fubmit to the vizier?

In general, original principles and feelings become paffive, if they are not, in their firft operation, confirmed by reafon and convictions of duty; and if the paffion which fprings up in their place affumes their appearance, and acts apparently as they would have done. Nothing is more impofing than this fpecies of ufurpation. It is not the open affault of a foe, but the guile of pretended friendfhip. Nothing

thing contributes more to dangerous felf-deception. Applying this remark to our prefent fubject, and following the lights of obfervation, we fhall briefly illuftrate, how early or inherent goodnefs may be fubverted by the love of diftinction. A perfon of good difpofitions, inclined by his temper and conftitution to perform acts of beneficence, receives pleafure in the performance. He alfo receives applaufes. He has done good, and is told of it. Thus he receives pleafure, not only from having gratified a native impulfe, but from the praife of mankind, and the gratitude of thofe whom he may have ferved. The applaufes he receives are more liberally beftowed by defigning and undeferving perfons, than by the deferving and undefigning. The deferving depend too much on the permanency of the original principle, independent of encouragement; and may therefore be too fparing in their approbation. Guftavus Adolphus

Adolphus ufed to fay, that valour needed encouragement; and was therefore un-referved in his praifes. The fame may be faid of every virtue. But defigning, or undeferving perfons, transferring their own difpofitions to other men, and of courfe apprehenfive left the wheels and fprings of benevolence fhould contract ruft, are oiling them for ever with pro-fufe adulation. Mean time, our man of liberality begins to be moved by other principles than fine feelings and confti-tutional impulfe. The pleafure arifing from fuch actions as thefe produce, is too fine and too delicate, compared with the joys conferred by loud and continued applaufes. Thus his tafte becomes vi-tiated; he not only acquires an undue relifh for adulation, but is uneafy with-out it; he contracts a falfe appetite; and folicits diftinction, not fo much for the pleafure it yields him, as to remove a difagreeable craving. Thus, fuch bene-

volent

volent actions as formerly proceeded from
conftitutional goodnefs, have now their
origin in the love of praife and diftinction. Goodnefs may remain in his breaft
a paffive gueft ; and having no other power
than to give countenance to the prevailing
principle. It may thus reign in his language
and reveries ; but the love of diftinction
directs his conduct. The fuperfeded mo-
narch enjoys the parade of ftate, and an-
nexes his fignature and fanction to the
deeds of his active minifter.

Perhaps it may now feem probable,
that a man of conftitutional goodnefs
may perform beneficent actions, not from
principles of humanity, though thefe
may actually refide in his breaft; but
from the defire of being diftinguifhed as
a generous perfon; and that in the mean
while, not difcerning his real motives,
he fhall imagine himfelf actuated by pure
generofity. That fuch characters may
exift, is all that is hitherto afferted. That
Shake-

Shakefpeare has exhibited an illuftration, accurately defined and exquifitely featured, in his Timon of Athens, we will now endeavour to fhew. We will endeavour to afcertain and trace, in the conduct of Timon, the marks of that beneficence which proceeds from the love of diftinction. We will, at the fame time, endeavour to trace the caufes of the ftrange alteration that took place in his temper; and delineate the operations of thofe circumftances that changed him from being apparently focial, and full of affection, into an abfolute mifanthrope.

I. Real goodnefs is not oftentatious. Not fo is the goodnefs of Timon. Obferve him in the firft fcene of the tragedy: trumpets found; Timon enters; he is furrounded with fenators, poets, painters, and attendants; chufes that moment to difplay his beneficence; and accompanies his benefits with a comment on his own noble nature.

I am

> I am not of that feather, to fhake off
> My friend when he moft needs me.

II. He is impatient of admonition. Knowing that he was formerly influenced by fentiments of humanity, he fuppofes that their power is abiding; and that, as he continues to do good, his principles of action are ftill the fame. He is expofed to this felf-impofition, not only by the tendency which all men have to deceive themfelves, but by the flatteries and praifes he is fond of receiving.— Of confequence, he would fuffer pain by being undeceived; he would lofe the pleafure of that diftinction which he fo earneftly purfues; the prevailing paffion would be counteracted: thus, there is a difpofition in his foul, which leads him to be difpleafed with the truth; and who that is offended with the truth, can endure admonition?

> Ap. Thou giv'ft fo long, Timon, I fear me, thou
> Wilt give away thyfelf in paper fhortly:
> What need thefe feafts, pomps, and vain glories?
>
> Tim.

Tim. Nay,
If you begin to rail once on fociety,
I am fworn not to give regard to you.
Farewell, and come with better mufic.
   Ap. So——
Thou wilt not hear me now.
——Oh, that men's ears fhould be
To counfel deaf, but not to flattery.

III. The fame felf-deceit which renders him deaf to counfel, renders him folicitous and patient of exceffive applaufe. He endures even the groffeft adulation. Notwithftanding the covering which hides him from himfelf, he cannot be quite confident that his principles are juft what he wifhes and imagines them to be. The applaufes he receives tend to obviate his uncertainty, and reconcile him to himfelf. Yet, it is not affirmed, that the man of confcious merit is either infenfible of fame, or carelefs of reputation. He feels and enjoys them both; but having lefs need of external evidence to ftrengthen him in the belief of his own integrity,

8   he

he is lefs voracious of praife, and more acute in the difcernment of flattery.

IV. The favours beftowed by Timon, are not often of fuch a kind as to do real fervice to the perfons who receive them. Wifhing to be celebrated for his bounty, he is liberal in fuch a manner as fhall be moft likely to draw attention, and particularly to provoke the oftentation of thofe, on account of his munificence, whom he is inclined to benefit. He is therefore more liberal in gratifying their paffions, and particularly their vanity, than in relieving their wants; and of contributing more to flatter their imaginations, than to promote their improvement. Though he performs fome actions of real humanity, and even thefe he performs in a public manner, yet his munificence appears chiefly in his banquets and fhewy prefents.

V. He acts in the fame manner, in the choice he makes of thofe whom he ferves, and

and on whom he confers his favours. He is not fo folicitous of alleviating the diftrefs of obfcure affliction, as of gratifying thofe who enjoy fome degree of diftinction, or have it in their power to proclaim his praifes. He is not reprefented as vifiting the cottage of the fatherlefs and widow; but is wonderfully generous to men of high rank and character. He is defirous of encouraging merit; but the merit muft be already known and acknowledged. In-ftead of drawing bafhful worth from ob-fcurity, he beftows coftly baubles on thofe eminent or reputable perfons who fhall be attended to, if they publifh his praifes. Thefe are fuch difplays of beneficence, as a man of genuine goodnefs would be apt to avoid. Yet, the perfons whom Timon honours and obliges, are loquacious poets, flattering painters, great generals, and mighty elders.

TIM. I take all, and your feveral vifitations,
So kind to heart, 'tis not enough to give;

G   Methinks

Methinks I could deal kingdoms to my friends,
And ne'er be weary. Alcibiades,
Thou art a foldier, therefore feldom rich;
It comes in charity to thee; for all thy living
Is 'mongft the dead; and all the lands thou haft
Lie in a pitched field.——

Yet, this feeming want of difcernment in Timon, is not to be confidered as a proof of weak underftanding. Our poet, who has omitted nothing to render the features of this character, though perhaps not obvious, yet fo diftinct, confiftent, and perfectly united, that there is fcarcely a lineament too little or too much, has guarded him from this objection, and reprefents him as a man of ability. When the ftate, and rulers of Athens, in the hour of extreme urgency and diftrefs, are threatened with an affault by Alcibiades, whom they had treated with difrefpect, they have recourfe for advice and affiftance to no other than Timon. They tell him in terms of humble entreaty:

There-

Therefore, fo pleafe thee to return with us,
And of our Athens (thine and ours) to take
The Captainfhip, thou fhalt be met with thanks,
Allow'd with abfolute power, and thy good name
Live with authority; fo foon fhall we drive back
Of Alcibiades the approaches wild,
Who, like a boar, too favage, doth root up
His country's peace.———

VI. Timon is not more oftentatious, impatient of admonition, defirous of applaufe, injudicious in his gifts, and undiftinguifhing in the choice of his friends, than he is profufe. Defirous of fuperlative praifes, he endeavours, by lavifh beneficence, to have unbounded returns.

————— He outgoes
The very heart of kindnefs———
——— ——— Plutus, the god of wealth,
Is but his fteward.

The poet, with judicious invention, deduces the chief incident in the play, namely the reverfe of Timon's fortune, from this circumftance in his conduct.

The

The vanity of Timon renders him profufe; and profufion renders him indigent.

VII. The character we are defcribing, fets a greater value on the favours he confers than they really deferve. Of a mind undifciplined by reafon, and moved by a ftrong defire, he conceives the ftate of things to be exactly fuch as his prefent mood and defire reprefent them. Wifhing to excite a high fenfe of favour, he believes he has done fo, and that the gratifications he beftows are much greater than what they are. He is the more liable to this felf-impofition, that many of thofe he is inclined to gratify, are no lefs lavifh of their adulation than he is of his fortune. He does not perceive that the raptures they exprefs are not for the benefit they have received, but for what they expect; and imagines, that while his chambers

Blaze with lights, and bray with minftrelfy;

while

while his cellars weep " with drunken
" fpilth of wine;" while he is giving
away horfes, and precious ftones; enter-
taining the rulers and chief men of
Athens, he fondly fancies that he is kind-
ling in their breafts a fenfe of friendfhip
and obligation. He fondly fancies, that in
his utmoft need, he will receive from them
every fort of affiftance ; and without referve or reluctance, lays immediate claim.
to their bounty.

> ———— You to Lord Lucius ;
> To Lord Lucullus, you—You to Sempronius :
> Commend me to their loves—and I am proud, fay,
> That my occafions have found time to ufe them
> Toward a fupply of money : let the requeft
> Be fifty talents.————
> Go you, Sir, to the fenators,
> (Of whom, even to the ftate's beft health, I have
> Deferved this hearing), bid them fend on th' inftant,
> A thoufand talents to me. .

VIII. Need we be furprifed that Timon,
and men of his character, fhould meet
with difappointment? Howfoever they

may

may impofe upon themfelves, and believe they are moved by real friendfhip, and believe that they are conferring real benefits, the reft of mankind difcern, and difapprove of their conduct. Even thofe very perfons, who, by adulation, and a mean acceptance of favours, have contributed to their delufion, feel, or conceive themfelves, under no obligation. The benefits they received were unfolicited, or unimportant; and the friendfhip of their benefactor was not fo genuine as he believed. Thus, then, Timon demands a requital of his good deeds: he meets with refufal; when he folicits the affections of his profeffing friends, he is anfwered with coldnefs.

> STR. Why, this is the world's fport;
> And juft of the fame piece is every flatt'rer's foul.
> ——Timon has been this Lord's father——
> He ne'er drinks,
> But Timon's filver treads upon his lip;
> And yet, (O fee the monftroufnefs of man,
> When he looks out in an ungrateful fhape),

He

He does deny him, in refpect of his,
What charitable men afford to beggars.

There is no one paffage in the whole
tragedy more happily conceived and expreffed than the conduct of Timon's flatterers. Their various contrivances to
avoid giving him affiftance, fhew diverfity of character; and their behaviour is
well contrafted, by the fincere forrow and
indignation of Timon's fervants. They
are held out to deferved fcorn, by their
eafy belief that the decay of their benefactor's fortunes was only pretended, and
by their confequent renewal of mean affi-
duities.

IX. It remains to be mentioned, that
fuch difappointment, in tempers like that
of Timon, begets not only refentment
at individuals, but averfion at all mankind.

Timon impofes on himfelf; and while
he is really actuated by a felfifh paffion,
fancies himfelf entirely difinterefted. Yet

G 4 he

he has no felect friends; and no particular attachments. He receives equally
the deferving and undeferving; the ftranger and the familiar acquaintance. Of
confequence, thofe perfons with whom
he feems intimate, have no concern in
his welfare; yet, vainly believing that he
merits their affections, he folicits their
affiftance, and sufgains difappointment.
His refentment is roufed; and he fuffers
as much pain, though perhaps of a different kind, as, in a fimilar fituation, a
perfon of true affection would fuffer.
But its object is materially different. For
againft whom is his anger excited? Not
againft one individual, for he had no individual attachment; but againft all thofe
who occafioned his difappointment: that
is, againft all thofe who were, or whom
he defired fhould be, the objects of his
beneficence; in other words, againft all.
mankind. In fuch circumftances, the
violence of refentment will be propor-

tioned

tioned to original fenfibility; and Shakefpeare, accordingly, has reprefented the
wrath of Timon as indulging itfelf in
furious invective, till it grows into lafting
averfion.

> TIM. Who dares, who dares;
> In purity of manhood ftand upright,
> And fay, this man's a flatterer? If one be,
> So are they all; for every greeze of fortune
> Is fmother'd by that below: the learned pate
> Ducks to the golden fool: all is oblique——
> ————Then be abhorr'd,
> All feafts, focieties, and throngs of men!
> His femblable, yea himfelf, Timon difdains;
> Deftruction phang mankind! Earth give me roots!
> Who feeks for better of thee, fauce his palate
> With thy moft operant poifon.

The fymptoms already mentioned are
numerous, and indicate to the attentive
obferver, that the ftate of Timon's mind
is more diftempered with a felfifh paffion
than he believes: yet the poet, by a de-
vice fuited to his own mafterly invention,
contrives an additional method of con-
veying

veying a diſtinct and explicit view of the
real deſign. Apemantus, a character well
invented and well ſupported, has no other
buſineſs in the play, than to explain the
principles of Timon's conduct. His cy-
nic ſurlineſs, indeed, forms a ſtriking contraſt to the ſmoothneſs of Timon's flatterers; but he is chiefly conſidered as un-
veiling the principal character. His manners are fierce; but his intentions are
friendly: his invectives are bitter; but
his remarks are true. He tells the flattering poet who had written a panegyric
on Timon, that he was worthy of him;
and adds, even in Timon's preſence, "He
"that loves to be flattered, is worthy of
"the flatterer." He tells Timon, in-
viting him to his banquet—"I ſcorn thy
"meat; 'twould choke me, for I ſhould
"ne'er flatter thee." Elſewhere he gives
him admonitions to the very ſame pur-
poſe; and finding his advice undervalued,
he ſubjoins — "I will lock thy heaven

9   "from

" from thee ;" meaning, as a commentator
has well explained it, the pleasure of being
flattered. He afterwards tells him, having
followed him, neverthelefs, into his folitude,
with intentions of rendering him some
affiftance ;

——————— What, thinkeft
That the bleak air, thy boift'rous chamberlain,
Will put thy fhirt on warm ? Will thofe mofs'd trees,
That have outliv'd the eagle, page thy heels,
And fkip when thou point'ft out ? Will the cold brook,
Candied with ice, caudle thy morning tafte,
To cure thy o'er-night's furfeit ? Call the creatures
Whofe naked natures live in all the fpite
Of wreckful heaven, whofe bare unhoufed trunks
To the conflicting elements expofed,
Anfwer mere nature—bid them flatter thee—
O ! thou fhalt find——

There are few inftances of a dramatic
character executed with fuch ftrict regard to unity of defign, as that of Timon.
This is not all. It is not enough to fay,
that all the parts of his conduct are confiftent, or connected with one general
prin-

principle. They have an union of a more intimate nature. All the qualities in his character, and all the circumſtances in his conduct, lead to one final event. They all co-operate, directly or indirectly, in the accompliſhment of one general pur- poſe. It is as if the poet had propoſed to demonſtrate, how perſons of good temper, and ſocial diſpoſitions, may be- come miſanthropical. He aſſumes the ſocial diſpoſitions to be conſtitutional, and not confirmed by reaſon or by re- flection. He then employs the love of diſtinction to bring about the concluſion. He ſhews its effects, in ſuperſeding the influence of better principles, in aſſuming their appearance, and ſo, in eſtabliſhing ſelf- deceit. He ſhews its effects, in producing oſtentation, injudicious profuſion, and diſ- appointment. And laſtly, he ſhews how its effects contributed to excite and exaſpe- rate thoſe bitter feelings which eſtranged Timon from all mankind. Timon, at

the

the beginning of the drama, feems altogether humane and affectionate; at the
end he is an abfolute mifanthrope. Such
oppofition indicates inconfiftency of character; unlefs the change can be traced
through its caufes and progrefs. If it
can be traced, and if the appearance fhall
feem natural, this afpect of the human
mind affords a curious and very interefting fpectacle. Obferve, in an inftance
or two, the fine lineaments and delicate
fhadings of this fingular character. The
poet refufes admiffion even to thofe circumftances which may be fuitable, and
confiftent enough with the general principle; but which would rather *coincide*
with the main defign, than *contribute* to its
confummation. Timon is lavifh; but he
is neither diffolute nor intemperate. He
is convivial; but he enjoys the banquet
not in his own, but in the pleafure of his
guefts. Though he difplays the pomp of
a mafquerade, Phrynia and Timandria are

in

in the train not of Timon, but of Alcibiades. He tells us, alluding to the correct-
nefs of his deportment,

> No villainous bounty yet hath pafs'd my heart;
> Unwifely, not ignobly, have I given.

We may obferve, too, that he is not fo
defirous of being diftinguifhed for mere
external magnificence, as of being diftinguifhed for courteous and beneficent actions. He does fome good, but it is to procure diftinction; he folicits diftinction, but
it is by doing good.

Upon the whole, " Shakefpeare, in his
" Timon of Athens, illuftrates the con-
" fequences of that inconfiderate profufion
" which has the appearance of liberality,
" and is fuppofed by the inconfiderate per-
" fon himfelf to proceed from a generous
" principle; but which, in reality, has its
" chief origin in the love of diftinction."

ESSAY

E S S A Y IV.

FAULTS OF SHAKESPEARE.

THE Commentators on Shakefpeare have been accufed of blind admiration. They are charged with over-rating his merits ; and of regarding his faults with exceffive indulgence. Only the laft part of the charge has a foundation in juftice. His merits have never been over-rated. The ardours of poetical fancy, the energies of ftrong expreffion, and unrivalled fkill in delineating human nature, belong to him in a degree fo confpicuous, as to juftify the warmeft applaufes, and even to excufe, in fome meafure, the indulgence fhewn him for his

tranf-

tranfgreffions. Yet his tranfgreffions are
great : nor have they paffed altogether
unnoticed. Foreign critics have affailed
him with virulence, and have loaded his
faults with the aggravations of national
prejudice. Even in Britain, the praife
of Shakefpeare is often mingled with lamentations for his offences. His inattention to the laws of unity, to fay nothing
of his deviations from geographical and
hiftorical truth; his rude mixture of tragic and comic fcenes; together with the
vulgarity, and even indecency of language, admitted too often into his dialogue, have expofed him to frequent cenfure. To cenfure him for his faults is
proper; it is even neceffary; it hinders
blind admiration from tainting the public
tafte; for offences againft tafte are more
dangerous in men of genius, than in other
perfons; and the undiftinguifhing praifes
fo profufely beftowed on Shakefpeare,

have

2

have contributed a good deal to retard our improvement in dramatical writing.

Is it then poffible, that a man of genius, eminently confpicuous in one of the higheft departments of elegant compofition, can trefpafs againft tafte; and contribute, even in fine writing, to pervert the judgment? Or is it likely that tafte and genius fhould depend upon different principles? They are, no doubt, a-kin; yet they are not fo clofely related, as that they may not be found apart. Many men, without poffeffing a fingle ray of invention, can difcern what is excellent in fine writing, and even feel its effects. But is it probable, that men of ardent fancy, of active invention, endowed with talents for various expreffion, and every power of poetical execution, are incapable, even in their own department, of perceiving, or feeling, what is fair or fublime? Shall the fpectator be ravifhed with unfpeakable tranfport; and fhall the breaft of him who communicates rapture be dark or joylefs? Such affer-

tion

tion is certainly bold; and though it feems implied in the charge againft Shakefpeare, it muft be heard with reftriction.

As every work that belongs to the imagination, all the performances of the poet, the painter, or ftatuary, confift of parts, the pleafure we receive from them is the effect of thofe parts acting in proper union. The general delightful influence of fuch combinations may be ftrongly felt, without our being able to diftinguifh their component members, whether of larger or of lefs dimenfion; or the nature of the relation fubfifting between them. Many tears have been fhed for the fufferings of Jane Shore and Califta; yet the perfons' who have fhed them may not have known by what art they were moved. We may alfo obferve, that the variety, the arrangement, the proportions, and mutual relations of thofe parts, which, united in a fine performance, afford us fupreme delight, may be feen and diftinguifhed by perfons, who,

from

from infenfibility natural or acquired,
•are incapable of feeling their influence,
or of perceiving them with exquifite pleafure. The accomplifhed critic muft both
feel what is excellent, and difcern its nature. Yet, there are critics who difcern,
and never feem to have felt. Eut, befides
feeling and difcernment, a certain portion
of knowledge is indifpenfably requifite:
for offences againft hiftorical, or obvious
philofophical truths, either in thofe that
perform a work, or in thofe that judge
of a performance, cannot fail of exciting
difguft. Thus, confummate tafte requires that we be capable of feeling
what is excellent; that we be capable,
in fome meafure, of difcerning the parts,
and correfpondence of parts, which, in
works of invention, occafion excellence;
and that we have competent knowledge in
thofe things which are the fubjects of an
artift's labour.

Now, every man of poetic invention
muft receive exquifite pleafure in con-

tem-

templating the great and the beautiful, both of art and of nature. He poffeffes tafte, in fo far as it depends upon feeling; and in fo far as a familiar acquaintance with beauty confers improvement, his tafte will improve. But he may want difcernment: for though the powers of difcernment are beftowed by nature, yet their perfection depends upon culture. He may not perceive proportion or union of parts in thofe things that give him pleafure; he may be totally ignorant of every fact concerning them, except in fo far as they work immediately on his fenfes; and thus, in fo far as tafte depends upon intellectual improvement, he is certainly defective. He may weep for the death of Laufus, as related by Virgil, without obferving that the fkill of the poet, in felecting and arranging thofe images that excite kindred emotions, is the magic power that affects him. He may be moved with an interefting ftory of a Bohemian Princefs, and not know

that

that no fuch Princefs exifted, or that Bo-
hemia is not, according to Shakefpeare's
reprefentation, a maritime country.—
Thus, with matchlefs pathetic abilities,
with uncommon ardour of fancy, and
force of expreffion, he may delineate the
fufferings of kings and of princes ; but by
miftaking hiftorical facts, and ftill more,
by blending incongruous emotions, he
may excite fuch difguft as fhall diminifh
the pleafure he would have given us ; and
occafion our regret, that his knowledge
had not been more extenfive, or his critical difcernment more improved.

But will not his feelings preferve
him from error? Will not their immediate and lively interpofition irradiate his
mind, and give him a clearer view of the
juftnefs and truth of things, than he can
receive from metaphyfical reafoning or
dry difquifition? Surely no feelings can
communicate the knowledge of facts ;
and though fenfibility of foul may difpofe
the mind to a readier difcernment of re-

lation

lation and connection, in the objects of
our attention, yet it is not by fenfibility
alone that we are capable of difcerning.
But allowing it to be fo; allowing that
there may be fome fpirits fo finely fram-
ed, that, with powers of active invention,
they can, independent of cool difquifition,
and without enquiring after union and
relation of parts, feel, by immediate impulfe, every effect of the moft exquifite
arrangement; and be able, by attending
to the degrees of pleafure they receive,
to afcertain the precife proportion, the
abundance, or defect of excellence, in a
work : admitting the poffibility of fuch
endowment, he who is thus highly diftinguifhed, is not, by means of this conftitution, exempt from error; he is not
placed beyond the rifk of misjudging,
nor rendered incapable of feeling amifs.
He cannot be fure of his feelings. They
are of a fhifting and verfatile nature.
They depend on the prefent humour, or
ftate of mind; and who can fay of the
                                    prefent

prefent humour, it will laft for a moment?
Who can affure us, efpecially if we afpire
at the honour of extreme fenfibility and
exquifite nerves, that our prefent mood
fhall not be totally different from that
which fhall follow? If fo, the colours
and attitudes of things fhall feem totally
changed: we fhall feel very different
emotions, and entertain very oppofite
fentiments. Could the man of genius
depend on his feelings; could he affure
himfelf that no contrary motions would
oppofe the natural tendencies of a delicate
fpirit; or, in particular, that the influence of fafhion fhould never efface from
his heart the true impreffions of beauty;
or that the authority of maxims, fpecious
or ill explained, fhould never pervert the
operations of fancy; he might proceed
with impetuous career; and, guided by
the pleafing irradiations of feeling, he
might fcorn the toil of that minute attention by which alone he might gain dif-

cernment.

cernment. Were there no adverfe currents, ftrong, but of filent progrefs; no
fhifting gales to drive him out of his
courfe, or no clouds to obfcure the face
of the fky, he might give full fcope to
his fails, and, obferving no other direction than the beams of fome bright con-
ftellation, he might proceed on a profperous voyage, and land at length on fome
blifsful ifland. But he has to encounter
oppofing currents, to contend with impetuous tempefts; his guiding ftar may
be involved in a ftorm, and his burnifhed
veffel may be dafhed upon rocks, or fhipwrecked on dangerous fands.

The man of true tafte muft not only
be capable of feeling, but of judging. He
muft afcertain his feelings. He muft diftinguifh thofe that are juft and natural,
from thofe that are fpurious. He muft
have fteady principles of judgment; and
eftablifh a rule of belief to which his
underftanding may for ever appeal, and
                                    fet

fet at defiance the effects of fleeting emotion. We are not always in the fame
ftate of mind; we are more fufceptible at
one time than another: even the fame
appearance fhall at different moments affect us differently; and we fhall be capable of relifhing at one time, what, in a
lefs happy mood, would have given us
no fort of pleafure. Nay, our fenfibility
may be, occafionally, not only dull, but
fickly; and we may be apt to find pleafure in thofe things, which, in themfelves, are neither wholefome nor inno-
cent. Add to this, that feelings of refpect for celebrated characters may be
as powerful in our minds as thofe of
beauty and harmony; or the authority of
a favourite critic may feduce us into er-
roneous opinions. Thus it is manifeft,
that trufting to feeling alone, our judgments may be capricious, unfteady, and
inconfiftent.

It is in morals as in criticifm. Our
judgments, and our conduct, muft be
eftablifhed

eſtabliſhed upon thoſe maxims that may have been ſuggeſted by feeling, but which muſt derive their force and ſtability from reaſon and deep reflection. We muſt have certain rules to direct our deportment, in thoſe moments of languor and dereliction, when the heart feels not the preſent influence of compaſſion, tenderneſs, and ſuch amiable diſpoſitions as produce excellent conduct. Thoſe celeſtial viſitants do not ſojourn continually in the human breaſt. Reaſon, therefore, and reflection, ought to preſerve ſuch tokens and memorials of their pleaſing intercourſe, as ſhall make us, in their abſence, act in full confidence that they are congenial with our nature, and will again return. By this due recollection, they will be induced to return; and, perhaps, to dwell in our breaſts for ever. But, without ſuch reſolutions; without acting as if we felt compaſſion and humanity, in the hope that we ſhall really

feel

feel them; and without rendering the sense of duty an established principle of action, we shall, in moments of feeble coldness, be not only feeble, but selfish; and not only cold, but inhuman. Our reason will be of no other service, than to assist or justify the perverse inclination; and a habit of callous insensibility may thus be contracted. It is needless to pursue the resemblance. It might easily be shewn, that in the conduct of life, no less than in our judgments concerning fine composition, if we have no determined principles, independent of present emotion, our deportment will be capricious, unsteady, and inconsistent *.

In particular, the man of mere sensibility, who has not established to himself, either in morals or in criticism, any rule of immutable conduct, and who depends on feeling alone for the propriety of his

judg-

* See the Essay on Lear.

judgments, may be mifled by the application of thofe general rules that direct
the conduct of others. His bofom is not
always equally fufceptible of fine emotion; yet, under the neceffity of acting
or of judging, and in a moment of dreary
dereliction, forfaken for a time by thofe
boafted feelings that are the guides of his
life, he will be apt to follow the fafhion;
or, apprehending that he is conducting
himfelf according to thofe well-eftablifh-
ed principles that influence men of worth,
he will be apt to fall into error. This
will be particularly the cafe, if any maxim
is held forth as a rule of conduct, proceeding upon rational views, and coinciding in general with the prepoffeffions of
fenfibility; but which requiring to be
attentively ftudied, well underftood, and
admitted with due extenfion, may, neverthelefs, be expreffed in fuch general terms,
with fo much brevity, and apparently of
fuch eafy comprehenfion, as that it is
often

often adopted without due extenfion; without being ftudied or underftood. Moreover, the warmeft advocate for the powers of feeling will allow, that they are often attended with diftruft, hefita- tion, and fomething like confcious weak- nefs. Hence it is, that perfons of mere fenfibility are ready to avail themfelves of any thing like a general maxim, which falls in with their own inclinations; and having no general maxim which is really their own, afcertained and eftablifhed by their own experience and reflection, they will be apt to embrace the dictates of others. Thus even an excellent rule, ill underftood, will confequently be ill ap- plied, and inftead of guiding men aright, will lead them into the mazes of error.

I am inclined to believe, and fhall now endeavour to illuftrate, that the greateft blemifhes in Shakefpeare have proceeded from his want of confummate tafte. Having no perfect difcernment, proceed-

ing

ing from rational inveſtigation, of the true cauſe of beauty in poetical compoſition, he had never eſtabliſhed in his mind any ſyſtem of regular proceſs, or any ſtandard of dramatic excellence. He felt the powerful effects of beauty; he wrote under the influence of feeling; but was apt to be miſled by thoſe general maxims, which are often repeated, but ill underſtood; which have foundation in truth, but muſt be followed with caution.

No maxim has been more frequently repeated, and more ſtrongly enforced upon poets, than that which requires them to " follow nature." The greateſt praiſe they expect is, that their repreſentations are natural; and the greateſt cenſure they dread is, that their conduct is oppoſite. It is by this maxim that the errors of Shakeſpeare have been defended; and probably by this maxim he was perverted. " Can we ſuppoſe," it may be

ſaid,

faid, " that the ruin of kings, and the
" downfal of kingdoms, have been ac-
" complifhed merely by heroes and
" princes? May not inferior agents, and
" even the meaneft of mankind, have
" contributed to fuch cataftrophe? Or
" can we fuppofe, that during the pro-
" grefs of great events, none of the real
" agents have ever fmiled, or have ever
" indulged themfelves in trifling dif-
" courfe? Muft they maintain, during
" the whole performance, the moft uni-
" form gravity of afpect, and folemn
" ftate of demeanour? Is it not natural,
" if a grave muft be dug for a dead body,
" that the grave-diggers be perfons of
" the loweft rank; and if fo, that their
" converfation be fuited to their condi-
" tion? Of confequence, the language
" of Tragedy will not always maintain
" the fame dignity of expreffion. Even
" kings and queens, moved by fome
" violent paffion, will be inclined to
" fpeak

" fpeak like their fubjects, and utter
" terms, that, to very delicate critics,
" may feem ill fuited to their rank. So-
" lemn ftatefmen may indulge in trivial
" garrulity; and grave fenators may act
" or fpeak like the vulgar. Now, is
" not the poet to follow nature? And if
" he is to reprefent perfons in the higheft
" departments of life, muft he not re-
" prefent them in their real appearance?
" Or muft they be totally difguifed, re-
" fined, and exalted, according to the en-
" thufiafm of a glowing fancy?"—It is
in this manner that the mixture of tragic
with comic fcenes, and the grofs vulgarity of language to which our poet,
notwithftanding his amazing powers of
expreffion, too often defcends, are defended; and, perhaps, as was already
mentioned, fome confiderations of this
fort have been the caufe of his errors.
Indeed, the facts in this fuppofed defence are admitted. Perfons of high
rank,

rank, in the execution of great under-
takings, may employ mercenary and vulgar engines; and may adapt their con-
verſation to the meaneſt of their aſſociates.
Mighty men may be coarſe and offenſive;
grave ſenators may, like ſome of thoſe
repreſented by Otway, be contemptibly
ſenſual; and even an Engliſh Princeſs,
agreeably to the repreſentation of Shakeſpeare, addreſſed by a deformed and loath-
ſome lover, may ſpit in his face, and call
him "hedge-hog." A Roman matron,
diſputing with the tribunes of the people,
who were perſecuting her ſon to death,
might with propriety enough have called
them "cats." A ſenator of Rome, in
the midſt of much civil diſſention, might
have ſaid of himſelf, that "he was a
"humorous patrician, and one that
"loved a cup of hot wine without
"a drop of allaying Tiber;" or in a debate with the above-mentioned tribunes,
he might tell them, that they, "racked

I "Rome

" Rome to make coals cheap;" or, with perfect confiftency of character, and truth of defcription, while, in a deep tragedy, he is delineating the referve of a difcontented general, he might fay of him, that " the tartnefs of his face fours ripe " grapes; that his hum is like a battery; " and that he fits in his ftate like a " thing made for Alexander." All thefe things may have happened, and as they may happen again, they may be termed natural. Yet, I conceive that the folemn, in dramatical compofition, fhould be kept apart from the ludicrous; that Shakefpeare, by confounding them, has incurred merited cenfure; and that he probably fell into error by following the authority of inexplicit, or unexamined decrees.

There is a certain confiftency of paffion, emotion, and fentiment, to be obferved in fine writing; not lefs important than unity of action, and of much greater

con-

confequence than the unities either of
time or of place. The mind is not only
pained by feelings difagreeable in themfelves, but, independent of their particular character and effect, it is pained by
being diftracted and haraffed. Now, this
difcompofure is produced, if oppofite
feelings, though in themfelves agreeable,
are poured in upon us at once, or in immediate fucceffion. As the tendency of
thefe diffonant emotions is to deftroy one
another, the mind, during the conteft,
is in a ftate of diftraction. Nor can
either of the contending feelings accomplifh their full effect; for the attention is
too equally divided between them, or
transferred fo rapidly from one object to
another, that the pleafure they would
yield is imperfect. Add to this, that in
cafes of fuch diforder, the finer feeling is
generally overpowered by the coarfer and
more tumultuous. A ludicrous character, or incident, introduced into a pa-

thetic

thetic fcene, will draw the chief attention to itfelf; and by ill-timed merriment, banifh the fofter pleafures. This fubject will receive more illuftration, if we attend to the fuccefs of thofe authors who have underftood and availed themfelves of the foregoing maxim. From this proceeds the chief merit of Milton's L'Allegro and Il Penforofo. Intending in his L'Allegro to excite chearfulnefs, he deals folely in chearful objects: intending in his Il Penforofo to promote a melancholy mood, he has recourfe to thofe images only that are connected with folitude and gloomy filence. If you would make us weep with compaffion, do not ftrive at the fame inftant to convulfe us with laughter. Or if you mean to exalt your audience with folemn and fublime devotion, you will not addrefs them with fantaftic levity, nor amufe them with a merry tune. The propriety of adhering to one leading idea, or in other words,

words, of moving the mind by one particular fet of feelings, has been attended
to in other imitative arts. We find nothing in mufic or painting, fo inconfiftent
as the diffonant mixture of fentiments
and emotions fo frequent in Englifh
tragedy. The improvers in gardening
are attentive to the fame obfervances.
They tell us, with great juftice, that in
a folemn fcene, every thing light and airy
fhould be concealed and removed; that
where fublimity conftitutes the chief expreffion, every circumftance fhould be
great or terrific; and, in general, that
all fubordinate incidents fhould be fuited
to the reigning character *. Even Shakefpeare himfelf, in many brilliant paffages,
where he follows the guidance of genius
alone, or of unperverted fenfibility, and,
indeed, in all thofe detached paffages that
are ufually mentioned as poffeffing fingu-

I 3   lar

---

* See " Obfervations on Modern Gardening," Sec. 50.

lar excellence, acts in perfect confistency with these observations. Every circumstance in his description of departed spirits, in " Measure for Measure," without suggesting noisome, disgusting objects, are directly calculated to fill the mind with delightful awe.

Now, if confistency of feeling and sentiment is to be observed in fine writing, it will affect our imitations of nature. It will lead us to bring more fully into view, than in the original, those things that carry forward, or coincide with, our purpose; and to conceal those circumstances which may be of an opposite or unsuitable tendency. If we would describe a chearful landscape, we will avoid mentioning the gloomy forests, or deep morasses, which may actually exist in it. In like manner, if we would dispose our audience to entertain sentiments of veneration for some respectable personage, we will throw into the shade those levities which may

have

have place in the character, but which leffen his dignity. In the fictions of the poet it is allowable, not only to veil infirmities, or to foften and conceal harfh or unbending features, but from the ftorehoufes of fancy and obfervation to make fuch additions, both to the landfcape and to the character, as fhall equally promote our pleafure and our efteem.

Does this rule, then, contradict the great maxim of following nature? Or is there any neceffity impofed upon us, of adopting the one and rejecting the other? If fo, to which fhall we yield the preference? We are not, however, reduced to this difficulty. We may both follow nature, not, indeed, as fervile copyifts, but as free difciples; and preferve at the fame time confiftency of feeling and expreffion.— When a judicious improver covers a bleak heath with enlivening groves, or removes the drearinefs of a noifome fen, by changing it into a lovely lake, inter-

I 4 fperfed

fperfed with iflands, can we accufe him
of departing from nature? Indeed he
varies her appearance, but at the fame
time improves them, and renders them
more agreeable to our conceptions of excellence. In like manner, the poet who
excludes from tragedy mean perfons and
vulgar language, becaufe they are diffonant
to the general tone of his work, neither
violates nature, nor trefpaffes againft the
great obligation he is under of affording us
pleafure.

Now, though the fpirit of this important rule has at all times operated on the
practice of eminent writers, and hath
even, on many occafions, influenced the
daring, but delicate fancy of Shakefpeare;
yet, in fo far as I recollect, the rule itfelf
has feldom been confidered by the authors
or judges of dramatic writing, in Britain,
as of inviolable obligation. Thus, the
maxim of following nature, a maxim moft
important in itfelf, and almoft coeval
with

with fine writing, has been received without proper extenfion: for it has commonly been conceived, that by the term
Nature, as ufed by the critics, we are to
underftand the real appearances of things
as they exift originally, and unimproved
by human art. According to this account, a tree with luxuriant branches,
and that has never been pruned, is natural. Neverthelefs, we may collect from
the foregoing remarks, that this ex-
planation is by far too limited. The
human mind is capable of difcerning and
conceiving excellence, fuperior to any
thing we have ever beheld. This excellence, however, does not belong to new
objects, but to the improved and exalted
ftate of thofe things with which we are
already acquainted. We cannot imagine
a new race of animated beings, different
in every refpect, except that of anima-
tion alone, from the living creatures that
we already know; but we can conceive

the

the prefent inhabitants of our planet exalted to a degree of perfection far fuperior to any of the human race. This idea
of excellence, therefore, is natural to the
human mind: the manner in which it is
formed may eafily be traced; and thofe
reprefentations of external things, which
differ from the real appearance, but coincide with our notions of improvement,
are to be held natural. This may receive
ftill farther illuftration. If by nature we
are to underftand the original, unimproved appearance of things, the wild
American favage is more according to nature than the civilized European. Yet,
will any one be bold enough to affirm,
that a mind highly improved and adorned
with fcience, is in a ftate that is unnatural? Neither fhall we fay fo of the tree
which is pruned and grafted, for the purpofe of bearing fruit; and which, left to
its original luxuriancy, would fhoot away
into ufelefs foliage. By the culture of
mind,

mind, and by the improvement of external objects, that excellence which we
conceive, is in part attained, and is held
to be according to nature. We cannot,
therefore, pronounce of that superior excellence which has not yet been attained, and which hitherto exists only in
idea, that it is unnatural. Now, the rule
of following nature having probably been
understood by Shakespeare in a sense too
limited, has betrayed him into those enormities that have incurred so much cen-
sure. Even his display of character has
sometimes been injured in its effect, by
this undeviating attachment to real appearance : and though, like Polonius,
statesmen and courtiers may, on various
occasions, be very wise and very foolish ;
yet, whatsoever, indulgence may be shewn
to the statesmen and courtiers of real life,
those of the drama must be of an uniform
and consistent conduct. Indeed, in co-
medy, there is nothing to hinder them
from

from appearing as ludicrous as in real life, or as the poet pleafes.

The other blemifhes in Shakefpeare are lefs enormous; and proceed chiefly from his want of critical and hiftorical knowledge; or from want of anxiety in correcting his works. Had he been well acquainted with the poets and critics of antiquity, he would probably have been more attentive to unity, and ftudied greater fimplicity in the form of his fables. Not that he would have adopted the practice of ancient poets, in its fulleft extent; for this would have been too oppofite to the public tafte, and too inconfiftent with his own luxuriant fancy. We may alfo add, that fome departure from the ftrict rules of unity enacted by ancient critics, and fome deviation from the fimplicity of Grecian poets, is no lofs to the drama. Shakefpeare, however, by having known them, and by having adhered to them in fome degree, would have been

been lefs irregular and incoherent. In like manner, by having been more acquainted with ancient hiftory, he would not have reprefented Alexander the Great as exifting prior to the age of Coriolanus; nor would he have reprefented the Roman matrons, in the days of Menenius Agrippa, as employing themfelves in fewing cambrick; nor would he have mentioned the tribunes of the Roman people as judges in the courts of juftice, or even at great pains to lower the price of coals; nor would he have infinuated that the Volfcians, either before or after eating, were accuftomed to fay grace.

Yet, glaring as thefe faults may appear, poets of no fmall reputation have been fo far feduced, by the example of Shakefpeare coinciding with the tafte of the times, that they have imitated, or at leaft not avoided, the very groffeft of his enormities. Otway and Southern are remarkable inftances. It may, therefore, be of fervice to the improvement of

fine

fine writing, not only to illuftrate the great merits of Shakefpeare, and to fhew in what manner his delineations of human nature may affift the philofopher; but alfo with candour, and the deference due to his fuperior genius, to have pointed out his defects, and endeavour to trace their caufes. In this inveftigation, the train of thought, independent of digref-fion or illuftration, is according to the following arrangement.

As the works of imagination confift of parts, the pleafure they yield is the ef-fect of thofe parts united in one defign. This effect may be felt; the relations of inferior, component parts, may be dif-cerned; and their nature may be known. Tafte is perfect, when fenfibility, dif-cernment, and knowledge, are united. Yet, they are not indifpenfably united in the man of poetic invention. He muft poffefs fenfibility; but he may want knowledge and difcernment. He will thus be liable to error. Guided folely by by feeling, his judgment will be unfteady; he will, at periods of languor, become the flave of authority, or be feduced by unexamined maxims. Shakefpeare was in this fituation. Endowed with genius, he poffeffed all the tafte that depended on feeling. But unimproved by the difcernment of the philofophical, or the knowledge of the learned critic, his fenfibility was expofed to perverfion. He was mifled by the general maxim that required him to "follow "nature." He obferved the rule in a limited fenfe. He copied the reality of external things; but difregarded that idea of excellence which feems inherent in the human mind. The rule, in its extended acceptation, requires, that objects intended to pleafe, and intereft the heart, fhould produce their effect, by correfponding or confonant feelings. Now, this cannot be attained by reprefenting objects as they appear. In every interefting reprefenta-tion, features and·tints muft be added to

3

the

the reality; features and tints which it
actually poffeffes, muft be concealed.
The greateft blemifhes in Shakefpeare
arofe from his not attending to this important rule; and not preferving in his
tragedies the proper tone of the work.
Hence the frequent and unbecoming mixture of meannefs and dignity in his expreffion; of the ferious and ludicrous
in his reprefentation. His other faults
are of lefs importance; and are charged
to his want of fufficient knowledge, or
care in correcting. In a word, though
his merits far furpafs thofe of every other
dramatic writer, and may even apologize
for his faults; yet, fince the ardour of
admiration may lead ingenious men to
overlook, or imitate, his imperfections,
it may be of fome fervice, " to point
" them out, and endeavour to trace their
" caufes."

ESSAY

E S S A Y V.

ADDITIONAL OBSERVATIONS

O N

SHAKESPEARE's

DRAMATIC CHARACTER

O F

H A M L E T;

IN A LETTER TO A FRIEND.

DEAR SIR,

I THANK you for your remarks on my account of Hamlet. Yet I frankly confefs, that notwithftanding their inge- nuity, I ftill adhere to my opinion* ; and

K   as

---

* Analyfis of Shakefpeare's Characters, p. 86, 3d Edit.

as I am folicitous that you fhould agree with me, I will, as briefly as poffible, lay my reafons before you. · Nor have I any doubt, but that the fame candour which dictated the objections, will procure attention to the reply. Allow me, then, to plead in behalf of Hamlet; and of Shake-fpeare *, if he need fuch aid; and of the Public, who, by always interefting themfelves in the fate of Hamlet, have, in this moft unequivocal manner, as on many other occafions, expreffed their approbation of Shakefpeare.

* * * * * *

The ftrongeft feature in the mind of Hamlet, as exhibited in the tragedy, is an exquifite fenfe of moral conduct. He difplays, at the fame time, great fenfibility of temper; and is, therefore, moft " tremblingly alive" to every incident or event that befalls him. His affections are

ardent,

---

* Si tali auxilio.

ardent, and his attachments lafting. He
alfo difplays a ftrong fenfe of character;
and therefore, a high regard for the opinions of others His good fenfe, and excellent difpofitions, in the early part of his
life, and in the profperous ftate of his fortune, rendered him amiable and beloved.
No misfortune had hitherto befallen him ;
and though he is reprefented to be fufceptible
of lively feelings, we have no evidence of
his having ever fhewn any fymptoms of
a morofe or melancholy difpofition. On
the contrary, the melancholy which throws
fo much gloom upon him in the courfe
of the play, appears to his former friends
and acquaintance altogether unufual and
unaccountable.

> ———— Something you have heard
> Of Hamlet's transformation : fo I call it;
> Since nor th' exterior, nor the inward man,
> Refembles that it was.

In the conduct, however, which he
difplays, in the progrefs of the tragedy,

he

he appears irrefolute and indecifive; he accordingly engages in enterprizes in which he fails; he difcovers reluctance to perform actions, which, we think, needed no hefitation; he proceeds to violent outrage, where the occafion does not feem to juftify violence; he appears jocular where his fituation is moft ferious and alarming; he ufes fubterfuges not con-fiftent with an ingenuous mind; and ex-preffes fentiments not only immoral, but inhuman.

This charge is heavy: yet every reader, and every audience, have hitherto taken part with Hamlet. They have not only pitied, but efteemed him; and the voice of the people, in poetry as well as poli-tics, deferves fome attention. Let us enquire, therefore, whether thofe parti-culars which have given fuch offence, may not be confidered as the infirmities of a mind conftituted like that of Hamlet, and placed in fuch trying circumftances, ra-

2   ther

ther than indications of folly, or proofs of inherent guilt. If so, he will still continue the proper object of our compassion, of our regret, and esteem. The award of the public will receive confirmation.

Consider, then, how a young person of good sense, of strong moral feelings, possessing an exquisite sense of character, great sensibility, together with much ardour and constancy of affection, would be apt to conduct himself, in a situation so peculiar as that of Hamlet. He loses a respectable father; nay, he has some reason to suspect, that his father had been treacherously murdered; that his uncle was the perpetrator of the cruel deed; and that his mother, whom he tenderly loved, was an accomplice in the guilt: he sees her suddenly married to the suspected murderer; he is himself excluded from his birth-right; he is placed in a conspicuous station; the world expects of him that he will resent or avenge his

K 3 wrongs:

wrongs : while in the mean time he is juftly apprehenfive of his being furrounded with fpies and informers. In thefe circum-ftances, and of fuch a character, if the poet had reprefented him as acting with fteady vigour and unexceptionable pro-priety, he would have reprefented not Hamlet, but a creature fo fanciful, as to have no prototype in human nature. We are not, therefore, to expect, that his con-duct is to proceed according to the moft infallible rules of difcretion or of propriety. We muft look for frailties and imperfec-tions ; but for the frailties and imperfec-tions of Hamlet.

I. The injuries he has fuftained, the guilt of Claudius, and the perverfion of Gertrude, excite his refentment, and in-dignation. Regard for the opinions of others, who expect fuch refentment in the Prince of Denmark, promotes the paffion. He therefore meditates, and re-folves on vengeance. But the moment

he

he forms his refolution, the fame virtuous fenfibility, and the fame regard to character, that roufed his indignation, fuggeft objections. He entertains a doubt concerning the ground of his fufpicions, and the evidence upon which he proceeds.

> ————— The fpirit that I've feen
> May be a devil; and the devil hath power
> T' affume a pleafing fhape; yea, and, perhaps,
> Out of my weaknefs and my melancholy,
> (As he is very potent with fuch fpirits),
> Abufes me to damn me. I'll have grounds
> More relative than this.

In this manner he becomes irrefolute and indecifive. Additionally, therefore, to the forrow and melancholy which he neceffarily feels for the fituation of his family, and which his peculiar frame of mind renders unufually poignant, the haraffment of fuch an inward ftruggle aggravates his affliction. His fenfe of duty, a regard to character, and feelings of juft refentment, prompt him to revenge: the

K 4   uncer-

uncertainty of his fufpicions, the fallacious nature of the evidence on which he proceeds, and the dread of perpetrating injuftice, embarrafs and arreft his pur-pofe.

> The time is out of joint—O curfed fpight,
> That ever I was born to fet it right.

This irrefolution, which indeed blafts his defigns, but does not leffen our regard for his character, nor our compaffion for his misfortunes, and the mifery with which it afflicts him, are pathetically defcribed and expreffed, in the famous foliloquy confequent to the reprefentation of the Players.

> What's Hecuba to him, or he to Hecuba,
> That he fhould weep for her? What would he do,
> Had he the motive and the cue for paffion
> That I have? &c.—Yet I, &c.

II. In that particular mood, when he fees his own wrongs and the guilt of Claudius in a ftriking light, his refentment

ment is inflamed, his evidence feems convincing; and he acts with a violence and
precipitation very diffimilar to, though
not inconfiftent with, his native temper.
In thefe circumftances, or at a time when
he tells us he

———Could drink hot blood!
And do fuch bitter bufinefs, as the day
Would quake to look on!

In fuch a fituation and ftate of mind, he
flew Polonius: he miftook him for the
king; and fo acted with a violence and·
precipitation of which he afterwards expreffes his repentences. In a fimilar fituation, when he had no leifure nor inclination to weigh and examine appearances, he
wrote the death-warrant of Rofencrantz
and Guildenftern.

Being thus benetted round with villanies,
Ere I could make a prologue to my brains,
They had begun the play: I fat me down,
Devis'd a new commiffion, &c.
An earneft conjuration from the king,

As England was his faithful tributary,
That on the view and knowing of thefe contents,·
He fhould the bearers put to fudden death.

Rofencrantz and Guildenftern had been employed as fpies upon Hamlet: under the difguife of friendfhip for him, they had accepted of this infamous office; they were in fome meafure acceffary to his intended affaffination: " they made love to " this employment;" and therefore, as " the defeat grew from their own infinu- " ation," there was no occafion why it " fhould fit near to Hamlet's confcience." If leifure had been given him to reflect, perhaps he would not have facrificed them; but having done the deed, he does not charge himfelf with deliberate guilt. He does not contend that his conduct was entirely blamelefs; he only tells us,

They are not *near* my confcience.

III. Thus agitated by external circum-ftances, torn by contending emotions,
                                        liable

liable to the weakneffes nearly allied to extreme fenfibility, and exhaufted by the contefts of violent paffions ; is it wonderful that he fhould exhibit dejection of mind, and exprefs difrelifh for every human enjoyment? This extreme is no lefs confiftent with his character than his temporary violence. " I have of late, " he tells Rofencrantz and Guildenftern, " loft " all my mirth ; forgone all cuftom of " exercifes ; and, indeed, it goes fo hea-
" vily with my difpofition, that this " goodly frame, the earth, feems to me " a fterile promontory; this moft excel-
" lent canopy, the air, look you, this " brave o'er-hanging firmament ; this " majeftical roof fretted with golden fire ; " why, it appears no other thing to me " than a foul and peftilent congregation " of vapours," &c. In like manner, the fame ftate of internal conteft leads him to a conduct directly oppofite to that of violence or precipitancy ; and when we expect

pect that he will give full vent to his refentment, he hefitates and recedes. This
is particularly illuftrated in the very difficult fcene where Hamlet, feeing Claudius kneeling and employed in devotion,
expreffes the following foliloquy:

Now might I do it pat, now he is praying;
And now I'll do it:—and fo he goes to heaven;
And fo am I reveng'd? That would be fcann'd,
A villain kills my father, and for that,
I, his fole fon, do this fame villain fend
To heaven.
Why, this is hire and falary, not revenge:
He took my father grofsly, full of bread,
With all his crimes broad blown, as flufh as May;
And, how his audit ftands, who knows, fave heaven?
But, in our circumftance and courfe of thought,
'Tis heavy with him: and am I then reveng'd,
To take him in the purging of his foul,
When he is fit and feafon'd for his paffage?

You afk me, why he did not kill the
Ufurper? And I anfwer, becaufe he was
at that inftant irrefolute. This irrefolution arofe from the inherent principles
of

of his conftitution, and is to be accounted natural : it arofe from virtuous, or at leaft from amiable, fenfibility, and therefore cannot be blamed. His fenfe of juftice, or his feelings of tendernefs, in a moment when his violent emotions were not excited, overcame his refentment. But you will urge the inconfiftency of this account, with the inhuman fentiments he expreffes :

Up, fword, and know thou a more horrid pent :
When he is drunk, afleep, or in his rage, &c.
Then trip him up, &c.

In reply to this difficulty, and it is not inconfiderable, I will venture to affirm, that thefe are not his real fentiments. There is nothing in the whole character of Hamlet that juftifies fuch favage enormity. We are therefore bound, in juftice and candour, to look for fome hypothefis that fhall reconcile what he now delivers, with his ufual maxims and general deportment.

portment. I would afk, then, whether, on many occafions, we do not alledge thofe confiderations as the motives of our conduct, which really are not our motives? Nay, is not this fometimes done almoft without our knowledge? Is it not done when we have no intention to deceive others; but when, by the influences of fome prefent paffion, we deceive ourfelves? The fact is confirmed by experience, if we commune with our own hearts; and by obfervation, if we look around. When the profligate is accufed of enormities, he will have them pafs for manly fpirit, or love of fociety; and impofes this opinion not upon others, but on himfelf. When the mifer indulges his love of wealth, he fays, and believes, that he follows the maxims of a laudable œconomy. So alfo, while the cenforious and invidious flanderer gratifies his malignity, he boafts, and believes, that he obeys the dictates of juftice. Confult

7

Bifhop

Biſhop Butler, your favourite, and the favourite of every real enquirer into the principles of human conduct, and you will be ſatisfied concerning the truth of the doctrine.—Apply it, then, to the caſe of Hamlet: ſenſe of ſuppoſed duty, and a regard to character, prompt him to ſlay his uncle; and he is with-held at that particular moment, by the aſcendant of a gentle diſpoſition; by the ſcruples, and perhaps weakneſs, of extreme ſenſibility. But how can he anſwer to the world, and to his ſenſe of duty, for miſſing this opportunity? The real motive cannot be urged. Inſtead of excuſing, it would expoſe him, he thinks, to cenſure; perhaps to contempt. He caſts about for a motive; and one better ſuited to the opinions of the multitude, and better calculated to lull reſentment, is immediately ſuggeſted. He indulges, and ſhelters himſelf under the ſubterfuge. He alledges, as direct cauſes of his delay, motives

that

that could never influence his conduct;
and thus exhibits a moft exquifite picture of amiable felf-deceit. The lines and
colours are, indeed, very fine; and not
very obvious to curfory obfervation. The
beauties of Shakefpeare, like genuine beauty of every kind, are often veiled; they
are not forward nor obtrufive. They do
not demand, though they claim attention.

IV. I would now offer fome obfervations concerning Hamlet's counterfeited
or real madnefs: and as they are alfo intended to juftify his moral conduct, let me
beg of you to keep ftill in view, the particular circumftances of his fituation, and
the peculiar frame of his mind.

- Haraffed from without, and diftracted
from within, is it wonderful, if, during
his endeavour to conceal his thoughts, he
fhould betray inattention to thofe around
him; incoherence of fpeech and manner; or break out inadvertently, into expreffions

preffions _of difpleafure? Is it wonderful
that he fhould "forego all mirth," become penfive, melancholy, or even morofe? Surely, fuch diforder of mind, in
characters like that of Hamlet, though
not amounting to actual madnefs, yet
exhibiting reafon in extreme perplexity,
and even trembling on the brink of madnefs, is not unufual. Meantime, Hamlet
was fully fenfible how ftrange thofe involuntary improprieties muft appear to
others : he was confcious he could not
fupprefs them ; he knew he was furrounded with fpies ; and was juftly apprehenfive, left his fufpicions or purpofes fhould
be difcovered. But how are thefe confequences to be prevented? By counterfeit-
ing an infanity which in part exifts. Accordingly, to Ophelia, to Polonius, and
others, he difplays more extravagance
than his real diforder would have occafioned. This particular afpect of the human mind is not unnatural; but is fo pe-

L   .culiar

culiar and fo exquifitely marked, that he alone who delineated the commencing madnefs, the blended reafon and diftrac-tion of Lear, hath ventured to pourtray its lineaments. That Hamlet really felt fome diforder, that he ftudied conceal-ment, and ftrove to hide his diftraction under appearances of madnefs, is manifeft in the following paffage, among others of the fame kind, where he difcovers much earneftnefs and emotion, and at the fame time, an affectation of fprightlinefs and unconcern :

Swear by my fword
Never to fpeak of this that you have heard.
   Ghost. Swear by his fword.
   Ham. Well faid, old mole! can'ft work i' the
     earth fo faft ?
A worthy pioneer! Once more remove, good friends.
   Hor. O day and night, but this is wond'rous
     ftrange !
   Ham. And therefore, as a ftranger, give it wel-
     come.
There are more things in heaven and earth, Horatio,
Than are dreamt of in your philofophy.——
                     But

But come ;——

Here, as before, never, fo help you mercy !

   GHOST. Swear, &c.

   HAM. Reft, reft, perturbed fpirit !

If we allow that the poet actually intended to reprefent Hamlet as feeling fome diftraction of mind; and was thus led to extravagancies which he affected to render ftill more extravagant, why, in his apology to Laertes, need we charge him with deviation from truth ?

This prefence knows, and you muft needs have heard,

How I am punifh'd with a fore diftraction.

What I have done,

That might your nature, honour, and exception,

Roughly awake, I here proclaim was madnefs.

Was't Hamlet wrong'd Laertes ? Never, Hamlet :

If Hamlet from himfelf be ta'en away,

And, when he's not himfelf, does wrong Laertes,

Then Hamlet does it not ; Hamlet denies it.

Hamlet, no doubt, put to death. Polonius; but without intention, and in the frenzy of tumultuous emotion. He might

     L 2   there-

therefore fay, both of that action and of the confequent madnefs of Ophelia,

> Let my difclaiming from a purpos'd evil,
> Free me fo far in your moft generous thoughts,
> That I have fhot my arrow o'er the houfe,
> And hurt my brother.

Neither is his conduct at the funeral of Ophelia to be conftrued into any defign of infulting Laertes.   His behaviour was the effect of violent perturbation ; and he fays fo afterwards, not only to Laertes, but to Horatio :

> ————— I am very forry, good Horatio,
> That to Laertes I forgot myfelf, &c.
> But fure, the bravery of his grief did put me
> Into a tow'ring paffion.

To this he alludes in his apology :

> If Hamlet from himfelf be ta'en away,
> And, when he's not himfelf, does wrong Laertes,
> Then Hamlet does it not ; Hamlet denies it.

The whole of his behaviour at the funeral, fhews a mind exceedingly diforder-

ed,

ed, and thrown into very violent agitation. But his affection for Ophelia appears fincere ; and his regard for Laertes genuine. On recovery from his tranfport, to which, however, Laertes provoked him, how pathetic is the following expoftulation :

> ————Hear you, Sir,
> What is the reafon that you us'd me thus ?
> I lov'd you ever.

I have been the more minute in confidering thofe particulars, that not only you, but Commentators of great reputation, have charged Hamlet, in this part of his conduct, with falfehood and inhumanity.

V. It remains that I fhould offer a few obfervations concerning Hamlet's jocularity. You feem to think it ftrange, that he fhould affect merriment when his fituation is miferable, and when he feels his mifery. Alas ! it is a fymptom, too un-

ambi-

ambiguous, of his affliction. He is fo miferable, that he has no relifh for any enjoyment; and is even weary of his exiftence.

> O that this too, too folid flefh would melt,
> Thaw, and refolve itfelf into a dew! &c.

Thinking himfelf incapable of happinefs, he thinks he fhould be quite unconcerned in any human event. This is another afpect of felf-deceit: for in truth he is not unconcerned. Yet acting as if it were fo, he affects to regard ferious, and even important matters, with a carelefs indifference. He would laugh: but his laughter is not that of mirth. Add to this, that in thofe moments when he fancies himfelf indifferent or unconcerned, he endeavours to treat thofe actions which would naturally excite indignation, with fcorn or contempt. This, on feveral occafions, leads him to affume the appearance of an ironical, but melancholy gaiety.

This

This ſtate of mind is exquiſitely delineated in the following paſſage, where his
affected melancholy betrays itſelf: and his
gaiety and indifference, notwithſtanding
his endeavours to preſerve them, relapſe
into his uſual mood.

> Hor. My Lord, I came to ſee your father's fune-
> ral.
> Ham. I pray thee, do not mock me, fellow ſtu-
> dent:
> I think it was to ſee my mother's wedding.
> Hor. Indeed, my Lord, it follow'd hard upon.
> Ham. Thrift, thrift, Horatio! the funeral bak'd
> meats
> Did coldly furniſh forth the marriage tables.
> Would I had met my deareſt foe in heaven,
> Or ever I had ſeen that day, Horatio.

From theſe remarks, I hope you will
now agree with me, that Hamlet deſerves
compaſſion; and that Horatio may ſay of
him, with propriety,

> ————Good night, ſweet Prince;
> And flights of angels ſing thee to thy reſt.

The

8

The character is confiftent. Hamlet is exhibited with good difpofitions, and ftruggling with untoward circumftances. The conteft is interefting. As he endeavours to act aright, we approve and efteem him. But his original conftitution renders him unequal to the conteft : he difplays the weakneffes and imperfections to which his peculiar character is liable ; he is unfortunate ; his misfortunes are in fome meafure occafioned by his weaknefs : he thus becomes an object not of blame, but of tender regret. Such a character would have appeared to Ariftotle peculiarly proper for theatrical reprefentation.

F I N I S.

E S S A Y S

ON

S H A K E S P E A R E ' S

DRAMATIC CHARACTER

OF

SIR JOHN FALSTAFF,

AND

ON HIS IMITATION

OF

FEMALE CHARACTERS.

To which are added,

SOME GENERAL OBSERVATIONS

ON THE

STUDY OF SHAKESPEARE,

BY MR. RICHARDSON,

Profeſſor of HUMANITY in the Univerſity of Glaſgow.

———————

L O N D O N:

PRINTED FOR J. MURRAY, Nº 32, FLEET-STREET.

M.DCC.LXXXVIII.

E S S A Y

O N

S H A K E S P E A R E'S

D R A M A T I C   C H A R A C T E R

O F

SIR JOHN FALSTAFF.

M Y intention in the following dif-
course, is to explain and account
for the pleasure we receive from the representation of Shakespeare's dramatic character of Sir John Falstaff. In treating this
subject, I shall with as much brevity as pos-
sible mention the cause on which our pleasure depends; and then by a particular ana-
lysis of the character endeavour to establish
my theory.

PART I.

No external object affects us in a more
disagreeable manner, than the view of suffer-

B   ing

ing occasioned by cruelty; our uneasiness arises not only from the display of calamity, but from the display of an inhuman mind. For how much soever human nature may exhibit interesting appearances, there are dispositions in mankind, which cannot otherwise be regarded than with abhorrence. Of this sort are cruelty, malice, and revenge. They affect us in the representation in the same manner as in real life. Neither the poet nor historian, if they represent them unmixed and unconnected with other ingredients, can ever render them agreeable. Who can without pain peruse the tragedy of Titus Andronicus, or the account given by Suetonius of the butcheries and enormities perpetrated by some of the Cæsars?

Yet with cruelty, malice, and revenge, many useful and even excellent qualities may be blended; of this kind are courage, independence of spirit, discernment of character, sagacity in the contrivance, and dexterity

terity in the execution, of arduous enterpri-
fes. Thefe, confidered apart, and unconnected with moral or immoral affections,
are viewed with confiderable pleafure, and
regarded with fome refpect. United with
good difpofitions, they produce the higheft
merit, and form the moft exalted character.
United with evil affections, though they do
not leffen, yet perhaps they counteract; at
leaft they alter the nature and tendency of
our abhorrence. We do not indeed, on
their account, regard the inhuman character
with lefs difapprobation; on the contrary,
our difapprobation is, if poffible, more determined. Yet, by the mixture of different
ingredients, our fenfations are changed;
they are not very painful; nay, if the proportion of refpectable qualities be confiderable,
they become agreeable. The character,
though highly blameable, attracts our notice, excites curiofity, and yields delight.
The character of Satan in Paradife Loft,
one of the moft finifhed in the whole range

of epic poetry, fully illuſtrates our obſerva-
tion: it diſplays, inhumanity, malice, and
revenge, united with ſagacity, intrepidity,
dexterity, and perſeverance. Of a ſimilar
kind, though with ſome different lineaments, is Shakeſpeare's King Richard the
Third; it excites indignation: indignation,
however, is not a painful, but rather an
agreeable feeling; a feeling too, which, if
duly governed, we do not blame ourſelves
for indulging.

We are led imperceptibly, almoſt by
every, and even by oppoſite bonds of aſſoci-
ation, by thoſe of contraſt and reſemblance,
to extend theſe remarks. There are qualities in human nature that excite abhorrence;
and qualities alſo that excite diſguſt. We
ſee ſome diſpoſitions that are enormouſly,
and ſome that are meanly, ſhocking. Some
give us pain by their atrocity, and ſome by
their baſeneſs. As virtuous actions may be
divided into thoſe that are reſpectable, and
thoſe that are amiable; ſo of vicious actions,

ſome

some are hateful, and affect us with horror; others are vile, and produce aversion. By one class, we have an imaginary, sympathetic, and transient apprehension of being hurt; by the other, we have a similar apprehension of being polluted. We would chastise the one with painful, and the other with shameful punishment. Of the latter sort are the gross excesses and perversion of inferior appetites. They hardly bear to be named; and scarcely, by any representation, without judicious circumlocution, and happy adjuncts, can be rendered agreeable. Who can mention, without reluctance, the mere glutton, the mere epicure, and the sot? And to these may be added the coward, the liar, the selfish and assenting parasite.

Yet the constituent parts of such characters may be so blended with other qualities of an agreeable, but neutral kind, as not only to lose their disgustful, but to gain an engaging aspect. They may be united

with

with a complaifance that has no afperity but that falls in readily, or without apparent conftraint, with every opinion or inclination. They may be united with good-humour, as oppofed to morcfenefs, and harfhnefs cf oppofition: with ingenuity and verfatility, in the arts of deceit: and with faculties for genuine or even fpurious wit; for the fpurious requires fome ability, and may, to fome minds, afford amufement. Add to this, that in fully explaining the appearance, in explaining how the mixture of different mental qualities, in the fame character, affords delight; we muft recollect, as on fimilar occafions, that when d fferent and even oppofite feelings encounter one another, and affect us at the fame time; thofe that prevail, under the guidance of fome vigorous paffion, carry the reft along with them; direct them fo as to receive the fame tendency with themfelves, and impelling the mind in the fame manner, receive from their coincidence additional

tional power *. They refemble the fwell
and progrefs of a Tartar army. One horde
meets with another ; they fight; the van-
quifhed unite with the victors : incorpo-
rated with them, under the direction of a
Timour or a Zingis, they augment their
force, and enable them to conquer others.

Characters of the kind above-mentioned,
confifting of mean and at the fame time of
agreeable qualities, regarded with difapprobation, are yet regarded with fome attention : they procure to themfelves fome attachment ; they excite neither fear, envy,
nor fufpicion : as they are not reckoned
noxious, the difapprobation they produce
is flight ; and they yield or promote amufement. What elfe are the race of parafites
both of ancient and modern times ?—the
gnathonici † of different forts, the direct and
indirect, the fmooth and the blunt ?—thofe
who by affentation, buffoonery, and even

* Hume's Effay on Tragedy.
† Terence.

B 4   with

wit, or fome appearance of wit, varied agreeably to the fhifting manners of mankind, relieve the fatigue of floth ; fill up the vacuity of minds that muft, but cannot think ; and are a fuitable fubftitute, when the gorged appetite loathes the banquet, and the downy couch can allure no flumbers ?

As perfons who difplay cruel difpofitions, united with force of mind and fuperior intellectual abilities, are regarded with indignation ; fo thofe whofe ruling defires aim at the gratification of grofs appetite, united with good-humour, and fuch intellectual endowments as may be fitted to gain favor, are regarded with fcorn. " Scorn, * like " indignation, feems to arife from a com- " parative view of two objects, the one " worthy, and the other unworthy, which " are neverthelefs united ; but which, on " account of the wrong or impropriety oc-

* Effay on Richard the Third.

" cafioned

" cafioned by this incongruous union, we
" conceive fhould be difunited and uncon-
": nected." The difference between them
feems to be, that the objects of indignation
are great and important, thofe of fcorn little
and unimportant. Indignation, of confequence, leads us to expreffions of anger:
but fcorn, as it denotes the feeling or difcernment of inferiority, with fuch mixture
of pretenfions as to produce contraft and
incongruity, is often expreffed by laughter;
and is, in a ferious mood, connected with
pity. Difdain is a-kin to indignation, and
implies confcioufnefs of inherent worth.
You difdain to act an unworthy part:

Difdain, which fprung from confcious merit, flufh'd
The cheeks of Dithyrambus.—   GLOVER.

Contempt does not fo much arife from
fuch confcioufnefs, as from the perception
of bafenefs in the object. To defpife, denotes a fentiment between difdain and contempt, which implies fome opinion of our

own

own fuperiority, and fome opinion of inferiority in the object; but neither in their
extremes *. Difdain, like indignation, is
allied to anger ; contempt, like fcorn, or
more fo, is connected with pity : but we
often defpife, without either pitying or being angry. When the meannefs, which is
the object of contempt, afpires by pretenfions to a connection with merit, and the
defign appearing productive of no great
harm, we are inclined to laugh : we are
moved with fcorn.

But in what manner fo ever we underftand the terms, for they are often con-
founded, and may not perhaps, in their
ufual acceptation, be thought to convey
the complete meaning here annexed to
them; the diftinctions themfelves have
a real foundation : and that which we
have chiefly in view at prefent, is fully il-

* Perhaps it denotes a kind of which difdain and
contempt are fpecies: we contemn a threat, we difdain an offer ; we defpife them both.

luftrated

luftrated in the character of Sir John Falftaff.   In him the effects arifing from the
" mixture of mean, grovelling, and bafe dif-
" pofitions with thofe qualities and difpo-
" fitions of a neutral kind, which afford
" pleafure ; and though not in themfelves
" objects of approbation, yet lead to at-
" tachment, are diftinctly felt and perceiv-
" ed."   In what follows of this difcourfe,
therefore, I fhall firft exemplify fome of
the bafer, and then fome of thofe agreeable
parts of the character that reconcile our
feelings, but not our reafon, to its deformity.

P A R T   II.

1. " The defire of gratifying the groffer
" and lower appetites, is the ruling and
" ftrongeft principle in the mind of Fal-
" ftaff."   Such indulgence is the aim of his
projects : upon this his conduct very uni-
formly hinges : and to this his other paffions
are not only fubordinate, but fubfervient.

His

His gluttony and love of dainty fare are ad-
mirably delineated in many paſſages ; but
with peculiar felicity in the following ;
where the poet diſplaying Falſtaff's ſenſu-
ality, in a method that is humorous and indirect ; and placing him in a ludicrous
ſituation, reconciles us by his exquiſite plea-
ſantry to a mean object.

" *Poins.* Falſtaff ! — faſt aſleep behind
" the arras : and ſnorting like a horſe.
" ——*P. H.* Hark, how hard he fetches
" breath ! Search his pockets. What
" haſt thou found ? —— *Poins.* Nothing
" but papers, my Lord.——*P. H.* Let's
" ſee what they be. Read them.——
" *Poins.* Item, a capon, 2 *s.* 2 *d.* Item,
" Sauce, 4 *d.* Item, Sack, two gallons,
" 5 *s.* 8 *d.* Item, Anchoves and ſack after
" ſupper, 2 *s.* 6 *d.* Item. Bread, a half-
" penny. —— *P. H.* O monſtrous ! but
" one halfpenny worth of bread to this in-
" tolerable deal of ſack !"——Who but
Shakeſpeare could have made a tavern-bill
the

the fubject of fo much mirth ; and fo happily inftrumental in the difplay of character ?

The fenfuality of the character is alfo held forth in the humorous and ludicrous views that are given of his perfon.

" *Falftaff.* The rafcal hath removed my " horfe, and tied him, I know not where. " If I travel but four feet by the fquare " further a-foot, I fhall break my wind. " Eight yards of uneven ground, is three- " fcore and ten miles a-foot with me : and " the ftony-hearted villains know it well " enough.——*P. H.* Peace, ye fat-guts ! " lie down, lay thine ear clofe to the " ground, and lift if thou canft hear the " tread of travellers. —— *Falftaff.* Have " you any levers to lift me up again, being " down ? S'blood, I'll not bear mine own " flefh fo far a-foot again for all the coin in " thy father's exchequer."

2. Purfuing no other object than the gratification of bodily pleafure, it is not
wonderful

wonderful that in fituations of danger, the care of the body fhould be his chief concern. He avoids fituations of danger: he does not wifh to be valiant; and without ftruggle or reluctance, adheres to his refolution. Thus his cowardice feems to be the refult of deliberation, rather than the effect of conftitution * : and is a determined purpofe of not expofing to injury or deftruction that corporeal ftructure, foul' and unwieldy tho' it be, on which his fupreme enjoyment fo completely depends. His well known foliloquy on honor difplays a mind, that having neither enthufiafm for fame, nor fenfe of reputation, is influenced in the hour of danger, by no principle but the fear of bodily pain: and if man were a mere fentient and mortal' animal, governed by no higher principle' than fenfual appetite, we might accede to his reafoning.—" Can honour fet a leg ? " No: or an arm? No: or take away

* Effay on Shakefpeare's Falftaff.

" the

" the grief of a wound? No: honour hath
" no fkill in furgery then? No."—Thus
while the fpeaker, in expreffing his real
fentiments, affects a playful manner, he affords a curious example of felf-impofition,
of an attempt to difguife confcious demerit,
and efcape from confcious difapprobation.

3. As perfons whofe ftrongeft principle
is the love of fame, are neverthelefs moved
by inferior appetites, and feek occafionally
their gratification; fo the fenfualift, conftructed originally like the reft of mankind,
may be fometimes moved by the defire of
praife or diftinction. Or, connecting this
defire, and the circumftance we have to
mention, more intimately with the ruling
power, we may fuppofe that he finds the
good-will, and confequently the good opinion, of his affociates, requifite or favorable
to his enjoyments, and may wifh therefore
to gain their regard. The diftinction, however, or efteem, to which he afpires, is not

for

for the reality, but the appearance, of merit:
about the reality, provided he appear mere-
torious, he is quite unconcerned.

4. Now this difpofition leads to pre-
fumption, to boaftful affectation and vain-
glory.—Falftaff is boaftful and vain-glorious. He wifhes, on many occafions, and
manifeftly for felfifh purpofes, to be reckoned a perfon of confummate and un-
daunted courage. He fpeaks of cowardice
with contempt, and affects the firmnefs or
confcious valour: " A plague of all cow-
" ards, I fay, and a vengeance too, marry
" and amen." He would alfo pafs for a
man whofe affiftance is of confequence,
or whofe favor deferves to be courted;
and in both thefe attempts he is fometimes, though not always, fuccefsful. His
hoftefs and Shallow may be impofed upon;
but he is better known to Prince Henry.—
Confiftently with, or in confequence of this
vain-glorious difpofition, whenever he finds
himfelf refpected, and that he is reckoned
a perfon

a perfon of fome importance, he affects
pride, becomes infolent, arrogant, and overbearing. It is in this manner he treats his
hoftefs, Bardolph, and other inferior affociates. " *P. H.* They take it already upon
" their falvation, that though I be but
" Prince of Wales, yet I am king of cour-
" tefy; and tell me flatly, I am no proud
" Jack, like Falftaff."

5. Falftaff is alfo deceitful: for the connection between vain-glorious affectation, and
unembarraffed, unreluctant deceit, is natural and intimate. He is deceitful in every
form of falfehood. He is a flatterer : he is
even hypocritical ; and tells the chief juftice
that he has " loft his voice finging an-
thems."

6. Shakefpeare intending to difplay the
magic of his fkill by rendering a mean character highly interefting, has added to it as
many bad qualities as, confiftently with
one another and with his main defign, can
be united in one affemblage. He accord-

C   ingly

ingly reprefents him, not only as a voluptuary, cowardly, vain-glorious, with all the
arrogance connected with vain-glory, and
deceitful in every fhape of deceit ; but inju-
rious, incapable of gratitude or of friendfhip,
and vindictive: The chief object of his life
being the indulgence of low appetite, he
has no regard for right or wrong ; and in
order to compafs his unworthy defigns, he
practifes fraud and injuftice. His attachments are mercenary : he fpeaks difrefpect-
fully of Prince Henry, to whofe friendfhip
he is indebted ; and values his friendfhip for
convenience rather than from regard. He is
alfo vindictive: but as he exprefles his re-
vengeful intention, without any opportunity
of difplaying it in action, his refentment becomes ridiculous. His menace againft the
chief Juftice, though illiberal and malicious,
is not regarded with indignation. One mode
of his vengeance is to defame thofe that
offend him by unwarrantable publications.
" He will print them," fays Page, fpeaking
about

about some of his ill-intentioned letters, " for he cares not what he puts into the " press."·

From the foregoing enumeration, it appears abundantly manifest, that our poet intended to represent Falstaff as very mean and worthless ; but, agreeably to an ingenious and peculiar method of unfolding the real character, and which he practises on some other occasions when he would obviate misapprehension, he embraces a good opportunity of making one of the most discerning personages connected with him, give the real delineation. Prince Henry has all along a clear and decided view of Falstaff ; and in the admirable scene where the King is personated as reproving his son, he thus describes him : " Thou art vio-" lently carried away from grace : there is " a devil haunts thee in the likeness of an. " old fat man : a tun of man is thy compa-" nion. Why dost thou converse with that " trunk of humours, &c. that stuff'd cloak-

" bag

" bag of guts, that roafted Manningtree ox
" with the pudding in his belly, that reve-
" rend vice, that grey iniquity, that vanity
" in years? Wherein is he good, but to tafte
" fack and drink it? Wherein neat and
" cleanly, but to carve a capon and eat it?
" Wherein cunning but in craft? Wherein
" crafty but in villany? Wherein villanous,
" but in all things? Wherein worthy, but
" in nothing?"—We have here the real
moral character; we have an enumeration of difguftful and bafe qualities, without a fingle circumftance to palliate or relieve. The fpeaker enlarges on his *fenfuality* as the leading feature in the character, and the principle on which every thing
elfe in his enumeration depends. How then
comes Falftaff to be a favorite? a favorite
with Prince Henry? and a favorite on the
Englifh ftage? For he not only makes us
laugh, but, it muft be acknowledged, is regarded with fome affection. The anfwer
to thefe enquiries leads us to our laft and
chief

chief divifion : it leads to illuftrate the affo-
ciated and blended qualities which not only
reconcile us to the reprefentation, but by
their mixture give us fingular pleafure.

P A R T III.

Thofe qualities in the charafter of Sir
John Falftaff which may be accounted ef-
timable are of two different kinds, the focial
and intellectual.

I. His focial qualities are joviality and
good-humour. Thefe difpofitions though
they are generally agreeable, and may in
one fenfe of the word be termed moral, as
influencing the manners and deportment of
mankind, are not on all occafions, as we
fhall fee exemplified in the prefent inftance,
to be accounted virtuous. They may be
agreeable without being objects of approbation. Perfons who have never given
much exercife to their minds, whofe powers of intellect and imagination languifh

through

through inexertion, can feldom have much enjoyment in being alone. He who cannot think, muft fly from himfelf; and, without having much regard for others, will feek relief in fociety. But as the bulk of mankind are not very inquifitive about the motives or caufes of thofe actions that do not intereft them very much, they are pleafed with fuch appearances of a relifh for focial intercourfe ; they are prepoffeffed in favor of thofe who court their fellowfhip, or who in their company difcover chearfulnefs and complacency.

Falftaff's love of fociety needs no illuftration; and that it is unconnected with friendfhip or affection is no lefs apparent. Yet the quality renders him acceptable.—— It receives great additional recommendation from his good-humour. As, amongft thofe whom he wifhes to pleafe, he is not fullen nor referved, neither is he morofe, nor apt to contradict or be offended. Perfons of active minds are moft liable to fuch exceffes. Whether

Whether they engage in the purfuits of fame, fortune, or even of amufement, they form fchemes, indulge expectation, are difquieted with folicitude, elated with joy, or vexed with difappointment. The activity of their fpirits expofes them to more occafions of difcompofure; and their fenfibility, natural or acquired, renders them more fufceptible of impreffions than other men. Hence, without careful difcipline or fteady refolution, they are apt to become uncomplying, violent, or impetuous. But the mere voluptuary is expofed to no fuch perverfion. He who never engages in ferious argument, who maintains no opinion, who contrives no intricate or extenfive projects, who is connected with no party, or concerned in no fpeculation, who has no intereft in any thing or any perfon beyond the gratification of mere appetite, has no object to contend for, nothing that can make him fo eager, fo tenacious, fo obftinate, or unyielding as perfons of a different character.

C 4 In

In such men, so slight a desire as that of being acceptable to some particular persons will, in their company, counterbalance every tendency to fretfulness, insolence, or ill-humour. Such seems to be the good-humour of Falstaff; for our poet discriminates with exquisite judgment, and delineates his conception with power. He does not attribute to Falstaff the good temper flowing from inherent goodness and genuine mildness of disposition; for in company with those about whose good opinion he has little concern, though his vacuity of mind obliges him to have recourse to their company, he is often insolent and overbearing. It is chiefly with Prince Henry, and those whom he wishes, from vanity, or some selfish purpose, to think well of him, that he is most facetious.—The degree or real force of any quality is never so distinctly marked, as when it is put to the test by such trying circumstances as tend to destroy its existence. Shakespeare seems aware of this; and, in the

first

firſt ſcene between the Prince and Falſtaff,
this part of the character is fully tried and
diſplayed. The Prince attacks Falſtaff in
a conteſt of banter and raillery. The
Knight for ſome time defends himſelf with
dexterity and ſucceſs. But the Prince's
jeſts are more ſevere than witty; they ſug-
geſt ſome harſh truths, and ſome well-
founded terrors.——" *P. H.* The fortune
" of us that are the moon's men, doth ebb
" and flow like the ſea, being governed as
" the ſea is by the moon : now in as low
" an ebb as the foot of the ladder; and by
" and by in as high a flow as the ridge of
" the gallows."——Such retorts are too
ſerious. The Knight endeavours to reply;
but he is overcome; he feels himſelf van-
quiſhed.

" *Falſtaff.* S'blood, I am as melancholy
" as a gib cat, or a lugg'd bear." But he
is not ſullen, nor moroſe. His melancholy,
as he terms it, does not appear in ill-humour, but in a laboured and not very ſuc-
cefsful

cefsful attempt to be witty. He is defirous of feeming in good fpirits, and embraces the firft opportunity given him by the Prince, of recovering them.——" *Falstaff.* " S'blood, I am as melancholy as a gib " cat or a lugg'd bear.——*P. H.* Or an " old lion, or a lover's lute.——*Falstaff.* " Yea, or the drone of a Lincolnfhire bag- " pipe.——*P. H.* What fayeft thou to a " hare, or the melancholy of Moor-ditch? " ——*Falstaff.* Thou haft the moft un- " favory fimilies, &c. But, Hal, I pray " thee, trouble me no more with vanity. " I would to God, thou and I knew where " a commodity of good names were to be " bought, &c. Thou haft done much " harm unto me, Hal; God forgive thee " for it! Before I knew thee, Hal, I knew " nothing; and now am I, if a man fhould " fpeak truly, little better than one of the " wicked, &c.——*P. H.* Where fhall we " take a purfe to-morrow, Jack?——*Fal-* " *staff.* Where thou wilt, lad, I'll make " one;

"one; an' I do not, call me villain, and
"baffle me."

II. Having fhewn that Falftaff poffeffes
as much love of fociety, and as much good-
temper as are confiftent with the defpi-
cable paffions of the fenfualift; and which,
though agreeable, are not in him to be accounted virtuous; I proceed to exemplify
his intellectual endowments : and of thefe
his talents for wit and humour are the
moft peculiar.

1. His wit is of various kinds. It is
fometimes a play upon words.—" *Falftaff.*
" I call thee coward ! I'll fee thee damn'd,
" ere I call thee coward. But I would
" give a thoufand pounds I could run as
" faft as thou canft. You are ftraight
" enough in the fhoulders. You care not
" who fees your back. Call you that
" backing of your friends ? A plague upon
" fuch backing! Give me them that will face
" me."——It fometimes depends on felicity of allufion.——" *Falftaff,*" to Bardolph,
"Thou

" Thou art our admiral, thou beareſt the
" lanthorn in the poop ; but 'tis in the noſe
" of thee. Thou art the knight of the
" burning lamp, &c. I never ſee thy face,
" but I think on hell-fire, and Dives that
" liv'd in purple, &c. O thou art a per-
" petual triumph, an everlaſting bonfire
" light : When thou ran'ſt up Gads-hill,
" in the night, to catch my horſe ; if I did
" not think thou hadſt been an ignis fatuus,
" or a ball of wild-fire, there is no pur-
" chaſe in money."——One of the moſt
agreeable ſpecies of wit, and which Falſtaff
uſes with great ſucceſs, is the ridiculous
compariſon.- It conſiſts in claſſing or unit-
ing together, by ſimilitude, objects that
excite feelings ſo oppoſite as that ſome may
be accounted great, and others little, ſome
noble, and others mean : and this is done,
when in their ſtructure, appearance, or effects, they have circumſtances of reſemblance abundantly obvious when pointed
out, though on account of the great difference

ference in their general impreſſion, not
uſually attended to ; but which being ſe-
lected by the man of witty invention, as
bonds of intimate union, enable him, by
an unexpected connection, to produce ſur-
priſe. Of this ſome of the preceding allu-
ſions, which are united with, or involve in
them compariſons, are inſtances : but the
following paſſage affords a more direct il-
luſtration.——" *Falſtaff*," ſpeaking of Shallow, " I do remember him at Clement's-
" inn, like a man made after ſupper with
" a cheeſe-paring. When he was naked,
" he was for all the world like a forked
" radiſh, with a head fantaſtically carved
" upon it with a knife."——Another very
exquiſite ſpecies of wit conſiſts in explaining great, ſerious, or important appearances, by inadequate and trifling cauſes *.
This, if one may ſay ſo, is a grave and ſo-
lemn ſpecies ; and produces its effect by
the affectation of formal and deep reſearch.

* Elements of Criticiſm.

Falſtaff

Falſtaff gives the following example : " A " good ſherris ſack has a two-fold opera- " tion : it aſcends me into the brain : dries " me there all the fooliſh, and dull, and " crudy vapours, which environ it : makes " it apprehenſive, quick, forgetive : full of " nimble, fiery, and delectable ſhapes ; " which delivered over to the voice (the " tongue) which is the birth, becomes ex- " cellent wit."

But Falſtaff is not more diſtinguiſhed for wit than humour : and affords ſome good illuſtrations of the difference between them. Wit conſiſts in the thought ; and produces its effect, namely laughter, or a tendency to laughter, in whatſoever way, and by whomſoever it may be ſpoken. Humour again depends on action : it ex- hibits ſomething done ; or ſomething ſaid in a peculiar manner. The action or the thing ſaid may be in themſelves indif- ferent ; but derive their power of exciting laughter from the intention and mode of

doing

doing or of faying them. Wit is permanent: it remains in the witty faying, by
whomfoever it is faid, and independent not
only of perfons, but of circumftances or
fituation. But in humour the action or
faying is ineffectual, unlefs connected with
the character, the intention, manner, or
fituation of fome fpeaker or agent. The
one feems to depend on connection, invented or difplayed unexpectedly, between
incongruous and diffonant objects, or parts
of objects: the other in the invention
or difplay of fuch connection between actions and manners incongruous to an occafion. The one prefents combinations
that may be termed ridiculous; the other
fuch as are ludicrous. The incongruity
and diffonance in both cafes feem chiefly
to refpect, not fo much the greatnefs or
littlenefs, as the dignity and meannefs, of
the connected objects. The amufement
is moft complete, when the witty thought
is exprefled with humour. When this is

*

not

not the cafe, though we difcern the witty combination, we do not feel its entire ef-fect. Among many others, the firft fcene between Falftaff and the Chief Juftice is highly humorous. It contains no wit in the beginning, which is indeed the moft amufing part of the dialogue : and the wit-ticifms introduced in the conclufion, ex-cepting the firft or fecond puns, are neither of a fuperior kind, nor executed with great fuccefs. The Juftice comes to reprove Falftaff : and the amufement confifts in Falftaff's pretending, firft of all, not to fee him ; and then, in pretending deafnefs, fo as neither to underftand his meffage, nor the purport of his converfation. ——" *Ch.* " *Juf.* Sir John Falftaff, a word with you. " ——*Falftaff.* My good lord ! God give " your lordfhip good time of day. I am " glad to fee your lordfhip abroad : I heard " fay your lordfhip was fick : I hope your " lordfhip goes abroad by advice. —— " *Ch. Juf.* Sir John, I fent for you, before

" your

" your expedition to Shrewfbury.——*Fal-*
"*ftaff.* If it pleafe your lordſhip, I hear
" his majefty is returned with fome dif-
" comfort from Wales.——*Ch. Juf.* I talk
" not of his majefty. You would not
" come when I fent for you.——*Fal.* And
" I hear, moreover, his highnefs is fallen
" into this fame whorefon apoplexy.——
" *Ch. Juf.* Well, Heaven mend him. I
" pray, let me fpeak with you.——*Fal.*
" This apoplexy is, as I take it, a kind of
" lethargy, an't pleafe your lordſhip; a
" kind of fleeping in the blood ; a whore-
" fon tingling. ——*Ch. Juf.* What tell you
" me of it ! be it as it is. ——*Fal.* It hath
" its original in much grief; from ftuiy,
" and perturbation of the brain," &c.——
The Chief Juftice becomes at length impatient, and compels Falftaff to hear and
give him a direct anfwer. But the Knight
is not without his refources. Driven out
of the ftrong hold of humour, he betakes
himfelf to the weapons of wit.——" *Ch.*

D   " *Juf.*

" *Juf.* The truth is, Sir John, you live in
" great infamy.——*Fal.* He that buckles
" himfelf in my belt cannot live in lefs.
" ——*Ch. Juf.* Your means are very flen-
" der, and your wafte great.——*Fal.* I
" would it were otherwife. I would my
" means were greater, and my waift flen-
" derer."——Falftaff is not unacquainted
with the nature and value of his talents.
He employs them not merely for the fake
of merriment, but to promote fome defign.
He wifhes, by his drollery in this fcene, to
cajole the Chief Juftice. In one of the following acts, he practifes the fame artifice
with the Prince of Lancafter. He fails,
however, in his attempt: and that it was
a ftudied attempt appears from his fubfequent reflections. " Good faith, this fame
" young fober-blooded boy doth not love
" me; nor a man cannot make him laugh."
That his pleafantry, whether witty or humorous, is often ftudied and premeditated, appears alfo from other paffages. " I
" will

" will devife matter enough out of this
" Shallow to keep Prince Henry in conti-
" nual laughter. O you fhall fee him
" laugh, till his face be like a wet cloak ill
" laid up."

It may alfo be remarked, that the guife
or raiment, fo to fay, with which Falftaff
invefts thofe different fpecies of wit and
humour, is univerfally the fame. It is grave,
and even folemn. He would always appear
in earneft. He does not laugh himfelf,
unlefs compelled by a fympathetic emotion
with the laughter of others. He may fometimes indeed indulge a fmile of feeming
contempt or indignation : but it is perhaps on no occafion when he would be
witty or humorous. Shakefpeare feems to
have thought this particular of importance,
and has therefore put it out of all doubt by
making Falftaff himfelf inform us ; " O it
" is much that a lie with a flight oath, and
" a jeft with a *fad brow*, will do with a fel-

" low that never had the ache in his fhoul-
" ders."

As the wit of Falftaff is various, and
finely blended with humour, it is alfo eafy
and genuine. It difplays no quaint con-
ceits, ftudied antithefes, or elaborate con-
trafts. Excepting in two or three inftances, we have no far-fetched or unfuccefsful
puns. Neither has the poet recourfe, for
ludicrous fituation, to frequent and difgufting difplays of drunkenefs : We have little
or no fwearing, and lefs obfcenity than from
the rudenefs of the times and the condition,
of fome of the other fpeakers we might have
expected.—Much ridicule is excited by
fome of the other characters : but their
wit, when they attempt to be witty, is different from that of Falftaff. Prince Henry's wit confifts chiefly in banter and raillery. In his fatirical allufions, he is often
more fevere than pleafant. The wit of
Piftol, if it be intended for wit, is altogether
affected,

affected, and is of a kind which Falſtaff never diſplays. It is an affectation of pompous language ; an attempt at the mock-heroic ; and conſiſts in employing inflated diction on common occaſions. The ſpeaker does not poſſeſs, but aim at wit ; and, for want of other reſources, endeavours to procure a laugh by odd expreſſions, and an abſurd application of learned and lofty phraſes.

> " Doſt thou thirſt, baſe Trojan,
> " To have me fold up Parca's fatal web ?"

Falſtaff's page being only a novice, attempts to be witty after the inflated manner of Piſtol : but being ſuppoſed to have profited by his maſter's example, he is more ſucceſſful, and his pompous phraſes have a witty meaning.——"*Page*" to Bardolph, "Away, " thou raſcally Althea's dream ! away!—— " *P. H.* Inſtruct us, boy ; what dream, " boy?——*Page.* Marry, my lord, Althea " dreamed ſhe was delivered of a fire-" brand ; and therefore I call him her

" dream."

" dream."——The laughter excited by the
reſt of Falſtaff's aſſociates, is not by the
wit or humour of the ſpeaker, but by
ludicrous ſituation, ridiculous views of peculiar manners, and the abſurd miſapplica-
tion of language. Thus in the admirable and
inſtructive account given by the hoſteſs of
Falſtaff's death—" Nay, ſure he's not in
" hell ; he's in Arthur's boſom, if ever man
" went to Arthur's boſom. He made a finer
" end, and went away an' it had been any
" Chriſtom'd child ; a' parted even juſt be-
" tween twelve and one, even at the turn-
" ing o' the tide : for after I ſaw him
" fumble with the ſheets, and play with
" flowers, and ſmile upon his finger's ends,
" I knew there was but one way ; for his
" noſe was as ſharp as a pen. How now,
" Sir John ? quoth I : what, man, be of
" good cheer : ſo 'a cried out, God, God,
" God, three or four times. Now I, to
" comfort him, bid him a' ſhould not think
" of God ; I hoped there was no need to
                                    " trouble

" trouble himfelf with any fuch thoughts
" yet : fo a' bade me lay more cloaths on
" his feet. I put my hand into the bed,
" and felt them; and they were as cold as
" a ftone; then I felt to his knees, and fo
" upward, and upward; and all was as cold
" as any ftone."

2. The other intellectual talents attributed by our poet to Sir John Falftaff, are
difcernment of character, verfatility, and
dexterity in the management of mankind;
a difcernment, however, and a dexterity of
a peculiar and limited fpecies; limited to
the power of difcerning whether or not men
may be rendered fit for his purpofes; and to
the power of managing them as the inftruments of his enjoyment.

We may remark his difcernment of mankind, and his dexterity in employing them,
in his conduct towards the Prince, to Shallow, and his inferior affociates.—He flatters
the Prince, but he ufes fuch flattery as is
intended to impofe on a perfon of under-

ftanding.

ſtanding. He flatters him indirectly. He ſeems to treat him with familiarity : he affects to be diſpleaſed with him : he rallies him ; and contends with him in the field of wit. When he gives praiſe, it is inſinuated ; or it ſeems reluctant, accidental, and extorted by the power of truth. In like manner, when he would impreſs him with a beief of his affectionate and firm attachment, he proceeds by inſinuation ; he would have it appear involuntary, the effect of ſtrong irreſiſtible impulſe ; ſo ſtrong as to appear preternatural. " If the raſcal hath not " given me medicines to make me love " him, I'll be hang'd." Yet his aim is not merely to pleaſe the Prince : it is to corrupt and govern him ; and to make him bend to his purpoſes, and become the inſtrument of his pleaſures. He makes the attempt : he ſeizes, what he thinks a good opportunity, by charging him with cowardice at the encounter of Gads-hill : he is deſirous of finding him a coward; puſhes

his

his attack as far as poffible; fuffers fudden repulfe: but with great verfatility and addrefs retires to his former faftnefs.——

" *Falftaff.* Are you not a coward? anfwer
" me that: and Poins there?——*P. H.*
" Ye fat paunch, an' ye call me coward,
" I'll ftab thee.——*Falftaff.* I call thee
" coward! I'll fee thee damned ere I call
" thee coward. But I would give a thou-
" fand pounds I could run as faft as thou
" canft, &c."——His behaviour to Shallow and Slender is different, becaufe their characters are different. He fathoms them, and fteers a correfponding courfe. He treats them at firft with fuch deference as he would render to men of fenfe and condition. He tries whether or no it be poffible to allure them by his ufual artifice; he is good-humoured, focial, and witty. But the wit he tries upon them is of his loweft kind: and he has no occafion for any other. They are delighted, and exprefs admiration.
" —— *Falftaff.* Is thy name Mouldy?
——" *Mouldy.*

" ——*Mouldy.* Yea, an't pleafe you.——
" *Falftaff.* It is the more time thou wert
" ufed.——*Shallow.* Ha! ha! ha! moft
" excellent, I'faith : things that are mouldy
" lack ufe. Well faid, Sir John, very well
" faid." He thus penetrates into their character, and conducts himfelf in a fuitable
manner. He no longer gives himfelf the
trouble of amufing them. He is no longer
witty : he affects the dignity of a great man,
and is fparing of his converfation. " I do
" fee the bottom," fays he, " of Juftice
" Shallow." Meanwhile Shallow and Slender become in their turns folicitous of pleafing *him :* they believe him a man of great
confequence : they think even of making
him *their* dupe, and of employing him as the
engine of their petty ambition. He indulges their folly, lets them entangle themfelves
in the fnare ; endures their converfation, and
does them the fignal honor of borrowing a
thoufand pounds.—His treatment of his
hoftefs and Bardolph is no lefs dexterous ;
but

but from the afcendant he has obtained, it is not fo difficult, and is managed by the poet in the moft inoffenfive manner.

3. Another kind of ability difplayed by our hero, is the addrefs with which he defies detection and extricates himfelf out of difficulty. He is never at a lofs. His prefence of mind never forfakes him. Having no fenfe of character, he is never troubled with fhame. Though frequently detected, or in danger of detection, his inventive faculty never fleeps ; it is never totally overwhelmed : or if it be furprifed into a momentary intermiffion of its power, it forthwith recovers, and fupplies him with frefh refources. He is furnifhed with palliatives . and excufes for every emergency. Befides other effects produced by this difplay of ability, it tends to amufe and excite laughter : for we are amufed by the application of inadequate and ridiculous caufes. Of the talent now mentioned we have many inftances. Thus when detected by Prince Henry

Henry in his boaſtful pretenſions to courage,
he tells him that he knew him. " Was it
" for me," ſays he, " to kill the heir-appa-
" rent ?" So alſo in another ſcene, when
he is detected in his abuſe of the Prince, and
overheard even by the Prince himſelf.
" No abuſe, Ned, in the world ; honeſt
" Ned, none. I diſpraiſed him before
" the wicked, that the wicked might not
" fall in love with him."—In the admirable ſcene where he is detected in falſely
and injuriouſly charging his hoſteſs with
having picked his pocket of ſome very valuable articles, whereas the theft was chiefly
of the ludicrous tavern-bill formerly mentioned, his eſcape is ſingularly remarkable.
He does not juſtify himſelf by any plea of
innocence. He does not colour nor palliate his offence. He cares not what baſeneſs may be imputed to himſelf: all that he
deſires is, that others may not be ſpotleſs.
If he can make them appear baſe, ſo much
the better. For how can they blame him,
if they themſelves are blameable ? On the

preſent

prefent occafion he has fome opportunity.
He fees and employs it. The Prince, in
rifling his pocket, had defcended to an un-
dignified action. The trefpafs indeed was
flight, and Falftaff could not reckon it
otherwife. But Prince Henry, poffeffing
the delicacies of honor, felt it with peculiar acutenefs. Falftaff, aware of this, employs the Prince's feelings as a counterpart
to his own bafenefs, and is fuccefsful. It
is on this particular point, though not ufually attended to, becaufe managed with
much addrefs, that his prefent refource depends.——" *P. H.* Thou fayeft true,
" Hoftefs, and he flanders thee moft grofsly.
" *Hoft.* So doth he you, my lord; and
" faid this day you ow'd him a thoufand
" pound.——*P. H.* Sirrah, do I owe you a'
" thoufand pound?——*Falftaff.* A thou-
" fand pound, Hal? a million : thy love is
" worth a million : thou oweft me thy love.
" ——*Hoft.* Nay, my lord, he called you
" Jack, and faid he would cudgel you.——

Falftaff.

" *Falstaff.* Did 1, Bardolph ?——*Bardolph.*
" Indeed, Sir John, you said so.——*Fal-*
" *staff.* Yea, if he said my ring was cop-
" per.——*P. H.* I say 'tis copper. Dar'st
" thou be as good as thy word now ?——
" *Falstaff.* Why, Hal, thou knowest, as
" thou art but a man, I dare ; but as thou
" art a Prince, I fear thee, as I fear the
" roaring of the lion's whelp.——*P. H.*
" And why not as the lion?——*Falstaff.*
" The King himself is to be fear'd as the
" lion ; dost thou think I'll fear thee as I
" fear thy father ? Nay, if I do, let my
" girdle break !——*P. H.* O, if it should,
" how would thy guts fall about thy knees !
" But, Sirrah, there's no room for faith,
" truth, nor honesty in this bosom of thine ;
" it is all filled up with guts and midriff.
" Charge an honest woman with picking
" thy pocket ! why, thou whoreson, impu-
" dent, imbossed rascal, if there were
" any thing in thy pocket but tavern reck-
" onings, memorandums of bawdy-houses,
" and

2

" and one poor penny-worth of fugar-
" candy to make thee long-winded ; if thy
" pocket were enriched with any other in-
" juries but thefe, I am a villain ; and yet
" you will ftand to it, you will not pocket
" up wrongs. Art thou not afham'd ?
" ―― *Falftaff.* Doft thou hear, Hal ?
" thou knoweft in the ftate of innocency
" Adam fell ; and what fhould poor Jack
" Falftaff do in the days of villany ? Thou
" feeft I have more flefh than another man,
" and therefore more frailty." Then he
adds, after an emphatic paufe, and no
doubt with a pointed application in the
manner : ―― " *You* confefs then that *you*
" picked my pocket ?" Prince Henry's
reply is very remarkable. It is not direct :
it contains no longer any raillery or reproach ; it is almoft a fhuffling anfwer, and
may be fuppofed to have been fpoken after,
or with fome confcious confufion :―" It
" appears fo," fays he, " from the ftory."
Falftaff pufhes him no further ; but expref-

fes

fes his triumph, under the fhew of modera-
tion and indifference, in his addrefs to the
hoftefs.——" Hoftefs, I forgive thee; go,
" make ready breakfaft; love thy hufband;
" look to thy fervants; and cherifh thy
" guefts: thou fhalt find me tractable to
" any honeft reafon: thou feeft I am paci-
" fied ftill."—I fhall illuftrate this particular
circumftance in one other inftance, not
only becaufe it is in itfelf curious; but tends
to elucidate what may, without impropriety,
be termed the cataftrophè. Falftaff having
impofed upon Shallow, borrows from him a
thoufand pounds. He has impofed upon
him, by making him believe that his influence with the Prince, now King Henry,
was all-powerful. Here the poet's good
fenfe, his fenfe of propriety, his judgment,
and invention, are indeed remarkable. It
was not for a perfon fo fenfual, fo cowardly,
fo arrogant, and fo felfifh as Falftaff, to triumph in his deceitful arts. But his punifhment muft be fuitable. He is not a
criminal

criminal like Richard ; and his recompence muſt be different. Detection, diſappointment in his fraudulent purpoſes, and the downfal of aſſumed importance, will ſatisfy poetical juſtice : and for ſuch retribution, even from his earlieſt appearance, we ſee due preparation. The puniſhment is to be the reſult of his conduct, and to be accompliſhed by a regular progreſs *.—Falſtaff, who was ſtudious of impoſing on others, impoſes upon himſelf. He becomes the dupe of his own artifice. Confident in his verſatility, command of temper, preſence of mind, and unabaſhed invention ; encouraged too by the notice of the Prince, and thus flattering himſelf that he ſhall have ſome ſway in his counſels, he lays the foundation of his own diſappointment. Though the flatterer and paraſite of Prince Henry, he does not deceive him. The Prince is thoroughly acquainted with his character, and

* Butler's Analogy.

E

is aware of his views. Yet in his wit, humour, and invention he finds amufement. —Parafites, in the works of other poets, are the flatterers of weak men, and imprefs them with a belief of their merit or attach- ment. But Falftaff is the parafite of a per- fon diftinguifhed for ability or underftand- ing. The Prince fees him in his real co- lours; yet, for the fake of prefent paftime, he fuffers himfelf to feem deceived; and al- lows the parafite to flatter himfelf that his arts are not unfuccefsful. The real ftate of his fentiments and feelings is finely defcribed, when at the battle of Shrewfbury, feeing Falftaff lying among fome dead bodies, he fuppofes him dead. " What! old ac- " quaintance! could not all this flefh " keep in a little life? Poor Jack, fare- " well. I could have better fpared a better " man : O I fhould have a heavy mifs of " thee, if I were much in love with va- " nity." But Prince Henry is not much in love with vanity. By his acceffion to the

the throne he feels himfelf under new obligations; and under the neceffity of relinquifhing improper purfuits. As he forms his refolution confiderately, he adheres to it ftrictly. He does not hefitate, nor tamper with inclination. He does not gradually loofen, but burfts his fetters. " He " cafts no longing lingering look behind." He forfakes every mean purfuit, and difcards every worthlefs dependent. But he difcards them with humanity: it is to avoid their influence, for all wife men avoid temptation; it is not to punifh, but to correct their vices.

> " I banifh thee, on pain of death,
> " Not to come near our perfon by ten miles!
> " For competence of life I will allow you,
> " That lack of means enforce you not to evil:
> " And as we hear you do reform yourfelves,
> " We will, according to your ftrengths and qua-
>   " lities,
> " Give you advancement."

Thus in the felf-deceit of Falftaff, and

in

in the difcernment of Henry, held out to us on all occafions, we have a natural foundation for the cataftrophe. The incidents too, by which it is accomplifhed, are judicioufly managed. None of them are foreign or external, but grow, as it were, out of the characters.

Falftaff brings Shallow to London to fee and profit by his influence at court. He places himfelf in King Henry's way, as he returns from the corona-.tion. He addreffes him with familiarity; is neglected; perfifts, and is repulfed with fternnefs. His hopes are unexpectedly baffled: his vanity blafted: he fees his importance with thofe whom he had deceived completely ruined: he is for a moment unmafked: he views himfelf as he believes he appears to them: he fees himfelf in the mirror of their conception: he runs over the confequences of his humiliation: he tranflates their thoughts and their opinions concerning him: he fpeaks

to

to them in the tone of the fentiments
which he attributes to them ; and in the
language which he thinks they would hold.
" Mafter Shallow, I owe you a thoufand
" pounds." It is not that in his abafe-
ment he feels a tranfient return of virtue :
it is rather that he fees himfelf for a moment helplefs : he fees his affumed importance deftroyed ; and, among other confequences, that reftitution of the fum he had
borrowed will be required. This alarms
him; and Shallow's anfwer gives him fmall
confolation. He is roufed from his fudden amazement: looks about for refources : and immediately finds them. His ingenuity comes inftantly to his aid ; and he
tells Shallow, with great readinefs and
plaufibility of invention, " Do not you
" grieve at this ? I fhall be fent for in pri-
" vate to him: look you, he muft feem
" thus to the world. Fear not your ad-
" vancement. I will be the man yet that
" fhall make you great, &c, This that

E 3   " you

" you heard was but a colour, &c. Go
" with me to dinner. Come, lieutenant
" Piſtol ; come, Bardolph ; I ſhall be ſent
" for ſoon at night."

Thus Shakeſpeare, whoſe morality is no
leſs ſublime than his ſkill in the diſplay of
character is maſterly and unrivalled, repreſents Falſtaff, not only as a voluptuous
and baſe ſycophant, but totally incorrigi-
ble. He diſplays no quality or diſpoſition
which can ſerve as a baſis for reformation.
Even his abilities and agreeable qualities
contribute to his depravity. Had he been
leſs facetious, leſs witty, leſs dexterous, and
leſs inventive, he might have been urged
to ſelf-condemnation, and ſo inclined to
amendment. But mortification leads
him to no conviction of folly, nor deter-
mines him to any change of life. He
turns, as ſoon as poſſible, from the view
given him of his baſeneſs ; and rattles as it
were in triumph, the fetters of habituated
and willing bondage.—Lear, violent and
impetuous,

impetuous, but yet affectionate; from his misfortunes derives improvement. Macbeth, originally a man of feeling, is capable of remorfe. And the underftanding of Richard, rugged and infenfible though he be, betrays his heart to the affault of confcience. But the mean fenfualift, incapable of honorable and worthy thoughts, is irretrievably loft; totally, and for ever depraved. An important and awful leffon!

I may be thought perhaps to have treated Falftaff with too much feverity. I am aware of his being a favorite. Perfons of eminent worth feel for him fome attachment, and think him hardly ufed by the King. But if they will allow themfelves to examine the character in all its parts, they will perhaps agree with me, that fuch feeling is delufive, and arifes from partial views. They will not take it amifs, if I fay that they are deluded in the fame manner with Prince Henry: They are amufed, and conceive an impro-

per

per attachment to the means of their pleafure and amufement. I appeal to every candid reader, whether the fentiment expreffed by Prince Henry is not that which every judicious fpectator and reader is inclined to feel.

" I could have better fpar'd a better man."

Upon the whole, the character of Sir John Falftaff, confifting of various parts, produces various feelings. Some of thefe are agreeable and fome difagreeable : but, being blended together, the general and united effect is much ftronger than if their impulfe had been difunited : not only fo, but as the agreeable qualities are brought more into view, for in this fenfe alone they can be faid to prevail in the character ; and as the deformity of other qualities is often veiled by the pleafantry employed by the poet in their difplay, the general effect is in the higheft degree delightful.

O N

'S H A K E S P E A R E'S

IMITATION OF

FEMALE CHARACTERS,

ADDRESSED TO A FRIEND.

I CANNOT agree with you, that Shakefpeare has exerted more ability in his imitation of male, than of female characters. Before you form a decided opinion on a fubject fo interefting to his reputation, let me requeft your attention to the following particulars. If you confider them at all, it will be with candour: and with fo much the more attention, that they are in favour of a Poet whom you admire, and, I might add, of a fex whom you adore. If Shakefpeare, with thofe embellifhments which we expect in poetry, has allotted to the females on his theatre fuch

ftations

ftations as are fuitable to their condition in
fociety, and delineated them with fufficient
difcrimination, he has done all that we have
any right to require. According to this
meafure, and this meafure alone, we are permitted to judge of him.—I will not, you
iee, be indebted to the facile apologift you
mention, who admits the charge; but
pleads in extenuation of the offence, that
Shakefpeare did not bring forward his female characters into a full and ftriking
light, " becaufe female players were in his
time unknown." His defence muft reft
upon critical principles: and if, " with
thofe embellifhments which we expect in
poetry, he has allotted to the females on
his theatre, fuch ftations as are fuitable to
their fituation in fociety; and if he has
delineated them with fufficient difcrimination, he has done all that we have any
right to require." I will now endeavour
to fhew, that he has fulfilled both thefe
conditions.

I. Diverfity

I. Diverſity of character depends a good deal on diverſity of ſituation : and ſituations are diverſified by variety of employment. We meet, for example, with leſs variety in the occupations of mankind in countries governed by deſpots, and unacquainted with trade and manufactures, than among nations that are free and commercial. The ſlaves of the deſpot diſplay no greater diverſity than depends upon the difference between poverty and riches : for their modes of education never affect the mind; they extend no farther than to ſuperinduce a varniſh of external urbanity; and confer ſome grace or pliancy in the management of the body. It would be a difficult enterprize, in a free country, to raiſe an illiterate and ignorant peaſant from the loweſt order to a diſtinguiſhed rank in the ſtate : but under ſome deſpotic governments, perſons with no other inſtruction than what regulates attitude, geſture, and ſome forms of external propriety, may

be

be exalted even to gorgeous pre-eminence.—If fituation influence the mind,
and if uniformity of conduct be frequently
occafioned by uniformity of condition ;
there muft be greater diverfity of male
than of female chai....ters. The employments of women, compared with thofe of
men, are few ; their condition, and of
courfe their manners, admit of lefs variety.
The poet, therefore, whether epic or dramatic, who would exhibit his heroines
in occupations that did not properly belong to them ; or who endeavoured to diftinguifh them by a greater diverfity of
habits, endowments, or difpofitions than
their condition juftified, would depart
from the truth of nature ; and, inftead of
meriting the praife of due decoration,
would incur the blame of extravagant
fiction. I fay not that the abilities and
difpofitions in both fexes may not be equal
or alike. There are few attainments in
knowledge in which the pride of the male

fex

fex may not be alarmed, if fuch alarm be decent, by the progrefs of fair competitors: and the hiftory of modern Europe will atteft, that even politics, a fcience of which men are particularly jealous, is not without the reach of adventurous females *. Difference, however, of condition reftrains the exertion of female genius ; and muft limit the difplay both of talents and difpofitions.

. Add to this, that the condition of women has been more reftrained in fome periods than in others. In times of great rudenefs, the wives † and daughters of the fierce barbarian are domeftic flaves. Even in civilized nations, if polygamy be permitted, and no reftraint impofed on the licentioufnefs of divorce, the fair-fex may

---

* The paths of criticifm alfo (as muft be well known to the lovers of Shakefpeare, who cannot be unacquainted with Mrs. Montague's Effay) have been fuccefsfully explored by female footfteps.

† Millar's Diftinction of Ranks.

be

be loved, if the paſſions of thoſe who grant themſelves ſuch indulgence may be honoured with the appellation of love ; but can never riſe to eſteem*. They may contribute to the amuſement or conveniency, but can never be the companions of men. In all ſituations whatever, where the tendency to extreme profligacy becomes very flagrant, the reſpect due to the female virtues, and confidence in female affection, decline and decay. So great are the obligations of the fair-ſex to thoſe inſtitutions, which, more than any other, by limiting the freedom of divorce, and by other proper reſtrictions, have aſſerted the dignity of the female character ! Poliſhed and even refined as were the manners of Athens and of Rome, the rank allowed to Athenian and Roman women was never ſo dignified, nor ſo ſuitable, in either of theſe republics, as among the nations of Chriſ-

---

* Και γαρ γυνη εςι χρηςτη και δυλος. Καιτοι γε ισως τυτων, το μεν χειρον, &c.   Ariſt. Poet.

tendom—

tendom.—But as the fubjects of dramatic poetry, and particularly of tragedy, are moft commonly furnifhed by rude, remote, or antient ages, the poet muft fubmit to fuch limitation, in his views of human life, as the manners of fuch periods require. And if Shakefpeare, like the great poets of antiquity, has not given his females fo much to do, or difplayed them as expreffing all the violence of paffion, or rendered them of fo much importance in the conduct of dramatic events, as may have been done by his brethren of later times ; he and the poets of antiquity have, in this inftance at leaft, given a more faithful, and not a lefs interefting reprefentation of that nature which they chofe to difplay.

II. I proceed ftill farther, and venture to affert, that there is not only as much variety in Shakefpeare's female characters as we have any title to demand ; but that they are diftinguifhed with peculiar and

appropriated

appropriated features. Let fome of them pafs in review before you. If you find in Miranda, Ifabella, Beatrice, and Portia, variety and difcrimination enough, they may anfwer for their numerous fifterhood: nor need we, on the prefent occafion, evoke the fpirits of Queen Margaret or Dame Quickly, Juliet or Defdemona.

1. In the character of Miranda, fimplicity is intended to be the moft ftriking circumftance. Confiftent, however, with fimplicity, is gentlenefs of difpofition, flowing out in compaffionate tendernefs, and unreftrained by fufpicion, Miranda, feeing the danger of fhipwrecked ftrangers, never fuppofes that they may be fuffering punifhment for heinous guilt, but expreffes the moft amiable commiferation:

" If by your art, my deareft father, you have
" Put the wild waters in this roar, allay them:
          " O I have fuffer'd
" With thofe that I faw fuffer."

Confcious

Conscious of no guile in herself, conscious of native truth, she believes that others are equally guileless, and reposes confidence in their professions. Her easy belief does not proceed from weakness; but from innate candour, and an ingenuous undismayed propensity, which had never been abused or insulted. If her simplicity and inexperience had rendered her shy and timid, the representation might have been reckoned natural: but Shakespeare has exhibited a more delicate picture. Miranda, under the care of a wise and affectionate father, an utter stranger to the rest of mankind, unacquainted with deceit either in others, or in herself, is more inclined to ingenuous confidence than to shy or reserved suspicion.—Moved in like manner by tender and ingenuous affection, she never practises dissimulation, never disguises her intention, either in the view of heightening the love or of trying the veracity of the person whom she prefers. All these particulars

F   are

are diftinctly illuftrated in the exquifite love-fcene between Ferdinand and Miranda.

" *Fer.* Admir'd Miranda,
" Indeed the top of admiration : worth
" What's deareft to the world ! &c.
    " *Mir.* I do not know
" One of my fex; no woman's face remember," &c.

Thus fimple, apt to wonder, guilelefs, and becaufe guilelefs of eafy belief, com-paffionate and tender, Miranda exhibits not only a confiftent, but a fingular, and finely-diftinguifhed character.

2. Ifabella is reprefented equally blame-lefs, amiable, and affectionate : fhe is particularly diftinguifhed by intellectual ability. Her underftanding and good-fenfe are confpicuous : her arguments are well-applied, and her pleading perfuafive. Yet her abilities do not offend by appearing too maf-culine : they are mitigated and finely blend-ed with female foftnefs. If fhe venture to argue, it is to fave the life of a brother.

Even

Even then, it is with such reluctance, he-
sitation, and diffidence, as need to be urged
and encouraged.

> " *Luc.* To him again, intreat him,
> " Kneel down before him, '&c.
> " *Isab.* O it is excellent
> " To have a giant's strength : but it is tyrannous
> " To use it like a giant.
> " *Luc.* That's well said."

The transitions in Isabella's pleadings are
natural and affecting. Her introduction is
timid and irresolute.

Lucio tells her,

> " If you should need a pin,
> " You could not with more lame a tongue desire it.
> " To him, I say."

Thus prompted, she makes an effort ; she
speaks from her immediate feelings : she has
not acquired boldness enough to enter the
lists of argument; and addresses him merely
as a suppliant :

> " Not the king's crown nor the deputed sword
> " The marshal's truncheon nor the judge's robe,
> " Become them with one half so good a grace,
> " As mercy does."

F 2   Animated

Animated by her exertion, she becomes more affured, and ventures to refute objections. As she is a nun, and confequently acquainted with religious knowledge, the argument she employs is fuited to her profeffion.

" *If.* Why, all the fouls that are, were forfeit once,
" And he that might the vantage beft have took,
" Found out the remedy."

At length, no longer abafhed and irrefolute, but fully collected, she reafons, fo to fay, on the merits of the caufe.

" Good, good, my lord, bethink you
" Who is it that hath died for this offence?
" There's many have committed it."

Nor is her argument unbecoming in the mouth even of a nun. Her fubfequent conduct vindicates her own character from afperfion. Befides, she had with great delicacy and propriety, at the beginning of her pleading, expreffed herfelf in fuch a manner, as to obviate any charge.

" There

" There is a vice that I do moſt abhor,
" And moſt deſire ſhould meet the blow of juſtice,
" For which I would not plead but that I muſt."

Emboldened by truth, and the feeling of good intention, ſhe paſſes, at the end of her debate, from the merits of the cauſe, to a ſpirited appeal even to the conſciouſneſs of her judge.

" Go to your boſom,
" Knock there, and aſk your heart what it doth know
" Like to your brother's fault."

Iſabella is not only ſenſible and perſuaſive, but ſagacious, and capable of becoming addreſs. In communicating to her brother the unworthy deſigns of Angelo, ſhe ſeems aware of his weakneſs; ſhe is not raſh nor incautious, but gives her intimation by degrees, and with ſtudied dexterity.

It is not inconſiſtent with her gentleneſs, modeſty, and referve, that, endowed as ſhe is with underſtanding, and ſtrongly impreſſed with a ſenſe of duty, ſhe ſhould

F 3   form

form refolutions refpecting her own conduct without reluctance, and adhere to them
without wavering. Though tenderly at-
tached to her brother, fhe fpurns, without
hefitation, the alternative propofed by Angelo, and never balances in her choice.

Neither is it incongruous, but a fine
tint in the character, that fhe feels indignation, and expreffes it ftrongly. But it is
not indignation againft an adverfary; it is
not on account of injury; it is a difinterefted emotion: it is againft a brother who
does not refpect himfelf; who expreffes
pufillanimous fentiments; and would have
her act in an unworthy manner.—Such is
the amiable, pious, fenfible, refolute, determined, and eloquent Ifabella. She pleads
powerfully for her brother; and no lefs
powerfully for her poetical father.

3. But if the gentle, unfufpecting, and
artlefs fimplicity of Miranda; if the good
fenfe and affecting eloquence of Ifabella,
fhould not induce you to acquit the poet,
you

you will yield, perhaps, to the vivacity and
wit of Beatrice.—No lefs amiable and affectionate than Miranda and Ifabella, fhe
expreffes refentment, becaufe fhe feels commiferation for the fufferings of her friend.
" Is he not approved in the height a vil-
" lain, that hath flandered, fcorned, and
" difhonoured my kinfwoman?" Like
Ifabella, too, fhe is diftinguifhed by intellectual ability ; but of a different kind.
She does not defend herfelf, or make her
attacks with grave, argumentative, and
perfuafive elocution ; but, endowed with
the powers of wit, fhe employs them in
raillery, banter, and repartee. " *Ben.*
" What, my dear Lady Difdain ! are you
" yet living ? — *Be.* Is it poffible Difdain
" fhould die, while fhe hath fuch meet food
" to feed upon, as fignor Benedict."—
" The count is neither fad, nor fick, nor
" merry, nor well ; but civil count, civil
" as a civil orange, and fomething of that
" jealous complexion."—Her fmartnefs,

however,

however, proceeds from wit rather than from humour. She does not attempt, or is not so succefsful in ludicrous defcription, as in lively fayings. " *Bea.* My coufin " tells him in his ear, that he is in her " heart.—*Claud.* And fo fhe does, coufin. " —*Beat.* Good lord for alliance! thus goes " every one to the world, but I, and I am " fun-burned; I may fit in a corner, and " cry heigh-ho for a hufband.—*Pe.* Lady " Beatrice, I will get you one.—*Beat.* I " would rather have one of your father's " getting."

Another diftinction, not unconnected with the preceding, is, that though lively, fhe is neverthelefs ferious, and though witty, grave. Poffeffed of talents for wit, fhe feems to employ them for the purpofes of defence or difguife. She conceals the real and thoughtful ferioufnefs of her dif-pofition by a fhew of vivacity. Howfoever fhe may fpeak of them, fhe treats her own concerns, and thofe of her friends, with

grave

grave confideration. A compliment, and the enticement of a playful allufion, almoft betrays her into an actual confeffion. " *Ped.* " In faith, lady, you have a merry heart. " —*Beat.* Yea, my lord, I thank it : poor " fool, it keeps on the windy fide of care." She is defirous of being reputed very fprightly and difdainful : but it is not of the qualities which we chiefly poffefs that we are ufually moft oftentatious. Congreve wifhed to be thought a fine gentleman ; Swift would be a politician ; and Milton a divine. What Beatrice, who is really amiable, would have herfelf thought to be, appears in the following paffage, where Hero, pretending not to know fhe was prefent, defcribes her in her own hearing.

" Nature never form'd a female heart
" Of prouder ftuff than that of Beatrice.
" Difdain and fcorn ride fparkling in her eyes,
" Mifprizing what they look on," &c.

Tender, affectionate, and ingenuous ; yet
confcious

confcious of more weaknefs than Miranda, or not like her educated in a defert ifland, fhe is aware of mankind, affects to be mirthful when fhe is moft in earneft, and employs her wit when fhe is moft afraid. —Nor is fuch diffimulation, if it may be fo termed, to be accounted peculiarly characteriftical of female manners. It may be difcovered in men of probity and tendernefs, and who are actuated by ferious principles ; but who are rendered timid, either from fome confcious imbecility ; or who become fufpicious by an early, too early an obfervation of defigning perfons. If fuch men are endowed with fo much livelinefs of invention, as, in the fociety to which they belong, to be reckoned witty or humorous, they often employ this talent as an engine of defence. Without it, they would perhaps fly from fociety, like the melancholy Jacques, who wifhed to have, but did not poffefs, a very diftinguifhed, though fome, portion of fuch ability.

Thus,

Thus, while they feem to annoy, they only wifh to prevent : their mock encounter is a real combat : while they feem for ever in the field, they conceive themfelves always befieged : though perfectly ferious, they never appear in earneft : and though they affect to fet all men at defiance ; and though they are not without underftanding, yet they tremble for the cenfure, and are tortured with the fneer of a fool. Let them come to the fchool of Shakefpeare. He will give *them*, as he gives many others, an ufeful leffon. He will fhew them an exemplary and natural reformation or exertion. Beatrice is not to be ridiculed out of an honorable purpofe ; nor to forfeit, for fear of a witlefs joke, a connection with a perfon who is " of a noble ftrain, of " approved valour, and confirmed ho-" nefty."

4. Portia is a-kin both to Beatrice and Ifabella. She refembles them both in gentlenefs of difpofition. Like Beatrice, fhe

is

is fpirited, lively, and witty. Her defcription of fome of her lovers, is an obvious
illuftration. " Firft, there is the Neapo-
" litan prince," &c. Her vivacity, however, is not fo brilliant, and approaches rather to fportive ingenuity than to wit. Her
fituation renders her lefs grave, when in a
ferious mood, than Ifabella : but, like her,
fhe has intellectual endowment. She is ob-
fervant, penetrating, and acute. Her addrefs is dexterous, and her apprehenfion extenfive. Though expofed to circumftances
that might excite indignation, fhe never
betrays any violent emotion, or unbecoming expreffion of anger. But Ifabella, on
account of her religious feclufion, having
had lefs intercourfe with the world, though
of a graver, and apparently of a more fedate
difpofition, expreffes her difpleafure with
reproach ; and inveighs with the holy wrath
of a cloifter. To the acquaintance which
both of them have of theology, Portia fu-
peradds fome knowledge of law ; and
                                    difplays

diſplays a dexterity of evaſion, along with an ingenuity in detecting a latent or uhob-ſerved meaning, which do her no diſcredit as a barriſter. We may obſerve too, that the principal buſineſs in the Merchant of Venice is conducted by Portia. Nor is it foreign to remark, that as in the intimacy of Roſalind and Celia, Shakeſpeare has re-preſented female friendſhip as no viſionary attainment; ſo he has, by the mouth of Portia, expreſſed ſome ſtriking particulars in the nature of that amiable connection.

> " In companions
> " That do converſe, and waſte the time together,
> " Whoſe ſouls do bear an equal yoke of love,
> " There muſt needs be a like proportion
> " Of lineaments, of manners, and of ſpirit."

5. Our poet, in his Cordelia, has given us a fine example of exquiſite ſenſibility, governed by reaſon, and guided by a ſenſe of propriety. This amiable character, in-deed, is conceived and executed with no leſs ſkill and invention than that of her fa-ther.

ther. Treated with rigour and injuftice by Lear, fhe utters no violent refentment; but expreffes becoming anxiety for reputation.

> " I yet befeech your majefty,
> " That you make known
> " It is no vicious blot, murder, or foulnefs,
> " No unchafte action or difhonor'd ftep,
> " That hath depriv'd me of your grace and favor."

She difplays the fame gentlenefs, accompanied with much delicacy of reproof, in her reply to a mercenary lover.

> " Peace be with Burgundy!
> " Since that refpects of fortune are his love,
> " I fhall not be his wife."

Even to her fifters, though fhe has perfect difcernment of their characters, and though her misfortune was owing to their diffimulation, fhe fhows nothing virulent nor unbecoming. She expreffes, however, in a fuitable manner, and with no improper irony, a fenfe of their deceit, and apprehenfions of their difaffection to Lear.

" Ye

I

" Ye jewels of our father, with wafh'd eyes
" Cordelia leaves you ; I know what you are,
" And like a fifter am moft loth to call
" Your faults as they are nam'd."

Towards the clofe of the tragedy, when fhe receives complete information concerning the violent outrages committed againft her father, the fufferings he has undergone, the ruin of his underftanding, and has the fulleft evidence of the guilt and atrocity of her fifters, fhe preferves the fame confiftency of character : notwithftanding her wrongs, fhe feels and is affected with the deepeft forrow for the misfortunes of Lear : fhe has the moft entire abhorrence of the temper difplayed by Goneril and Regan : yet her forrows, her refentment, and indignation are guided by that fenfe of propriety, which does not in the fmalleft degree impair her tendernefs and fenfibility ; but directs them to that conduct and demeanour, which are fuitable, amiable, and interefting. Tendernefs, affection, and fenfibility, melting into grief, and mingled with fentiments

of

of reluctant difapprobation, were never delineated with more delicacy than in the
defcription of Cordelia, when fhe receives
intelligence of her father's misfortunes.

" *Kent.* Did your letters pierce the queen ? any de-
" monftration of grief ?

" *Gent.* I fay fhe took 'em, read 'em in my prefence;
" And now and then an ample tear trill'd down
" Her delicate cheek : it feem'd fhe was a queen
" Over her paffion, which moft rebel like
" Sought to be king over her."

" *Kent.* O then it moved her.

" *Gent.* But no rage. Patience and forrow ftrove
" Which fhould exprefs her goodlieft : you have feen
" Sun-fhine and rain at once. Thofe happieft fmiles
" That played on her ripe lip feem'd not to know
" What guefts were in her eyes, which parted thence,
" As pearls from diamonds dropt.—In brief,
" Sorrow would be a rarity moft belov'd,
" If all could fo become it."

" *Kent.* Made fhe no verbal queftion ?

" *Gent.* Once or twice
" She heav'd the name of father
" Pantingly forth, as if it preft her heart,
" Cry'd, Sifters ! Sifters ! What ? i'th' ftorm of night?
" Let pity ne'er believe it ! then fhe fhook

" The

" The holy water from her heav'nly eyes,
" And then retir'd to deal with grief alone."

Minds highly enlightened, contemplating the fame object, both reafon and are
affected in a fimilar manner. The tone of
thought in the following paffage, in ' The
' Theory of Moral Sentiments,' accords
perfectly with Shakefpeare's account of
Cordelia. ' What noble propriety and
grace do we feel in the conduct of thofe
who, in their own cafe, exert that recollection and felf-command which conftitute
the dignity of every paffion, and which
bring it down to what others can enter
into? We are difgufted with that clamor-
ous grief, which, without any delicacy,
calls upon our compaffion with fighs and
importunate lamentations. But we reve-
rence that referved, that filent and ma-
jeftic forrow, which difcovers itfelf only in
the fwelling of the eyes, in the quivering
of the lips and cheeks, and in the diftant
but affecting coldnefs of the whole beha-

G   viour.

viour. It impofes the like filence upon
us. We regard it with refpectful attention,
and watch with anxious concern over our
whole behaviour, left by any impropriety
we fhould difturb that concerted tranquil-
lity, which it requires fo great an effort to
fupport.'—Cordelia, full of affection, feels
for the diftrefs of her father: her fenfe of
propriety impofes reftraint on her expreffions of forrow: the conflict is painful: full of fenfibility, and of a delicate
ftructure; the conflict is more than fhe can
endure; fhe muft indulge her emotions:
her fenfe of propriety again interpofes; fhe
muft vent them in fecret, and not with
loud lamentation.

" She fhakes
" The holy water from her heavenly eyes,
" And then retires to deal with grief alone."

There are few inftances in any poet,
where the influences of contending emotions are fo nicely balanced and diftinguifhed: for while in this amiable picture we difcern the corrected feverity of

that

that behaviour which a fenfe of propriety dictates, mitigated and brought down by fine fenfibility, and the foftnefs of the female character; we alfo fee this foftnefs upheld, and this fenfibility rendered ftill more engaging, by the influences of a fenfe of propriety.

Need I add to thefe illuftrations, the fifterly and filial affections of Ophelia, leading her to fuch deference for a father, as to practife deceit at his fuggeftion on a generous lover, and ftrive to entangle him in the toils of political cunning? Need I add the pride, the violence, the abilities, and the difappointed ambition of Margaret? Need I add Dame Quickly and Lady Anne?—If, notwithftanding all thefe, you perfift in faying that Shakefpeare has produced no eminent female characters, becaufe, in the words of the poet whom you quote ' moft women have no character at all;' you muft mean in the fpirit or manner of the fatirift, and with an eye to the perfonage laftmentioned, to pun rather than to refute.

But

But you tell me—" the gentle Defdemona is like the gentle Cordelia ; the tender Imogen like the tender Juliet ; the
fenfible Ifabella like the fenfible Portia ;
the violent Margaret like the violent
Conftance ; and the cruel Regan like
the cruel Goneril : in fhort, that they
are all copies of one another ; that
any differences appearing between them
are occafioned by difference of external
circumftances ; that Portia, in Ifabella's
fituation, would have been another Ifabella : and fo with the reft."—If this be
urged as an objection, it cannot be admitted. Defdemona, in the fame fituation
with Margaret, would not have inveighed,
nor vented imprecation. Cordelia was
fituated in the fame circumftances with
Regan, but performed a very different
part. Notwithftanding the fimilarity in
the inftances above-mentioned, there is ftill
fo much diverfity as to obviate the objection.—Still further, if you reafon in this
manner, allow me to fay, in the words of

the

the poet, you reafon " too curioufly:"
and would reduce the fum of dramatic
characters, how different foever their names
and fortunes, to an inconfiderable number. Does it not ftrike you, too, that to
difregard fuch difcrimination as proceeds
from external condition, is contrary to the
truth of nature, and the juftice of impar-
tial criticifm? Many perfons may have
received from nature fimilar talents and
difpofitions; but being differently placed
in fociety, they exert the fame power, or
gratify the fame defire, with different degrees of force, and different modes of indulgence. Their characters are therefore
different, and if fo in reality, fo alfo in imitation. Similarity of original ftructure
does not conftitute fimilarity or famenefs
of character, unlefs that fimilarity appear
in the fame circumftances, in the fame
manner, and with equal force. I ftill
therefore adhere to my former opinion :
and have not ventured, I hope, in vain to
affert the merits of Shakefpeare's females.

OBSERVATIONS

ON THE

CHIEF OBJECTS of CRITICISM

IN THE WORKS OF

SHAKESPEARE.

NO poetical writer among the moderns has afforded more employment to critics and commentators than Shakespeare. As he wrote while the manners, no less than the language, of his countrymen, were very different from what they are at present; and as he is reported to have been very careless about the fate of his performances after they were given to the public, he is become in many instances difficult, and almost unintelligible. Hence several learned and

discerning

difcerning editors have rendered effential fervice to the literature of their country, by explaining his obfolete phrafes, by freeing his text from fpurious paffages, and by elucidating his frequent allufions to obfcure or antiquated cuftoms. Labours of this fort are fo much the more valuable, as Shakefpeare is juftly accounted the great poet of human nature. Even to moralifts and philofophers, his difplay and illuftration of paffions and manners, may afford not only amufement, but inftruction.

" The operations of the mind," as has been well obferved by an anonymous writer, in his remarks on fome of the preceding effays, " are more complex " than thofe of the body : its motions are " progreffive: its tranfitions abrupt and " inftantaneous: its attitudes uncertain " and momentary. The paffions purfue " their courfe with celerity ; their direc- " tion may be changed, or their impetu-

G 4   " ofity

" ofity modified by a number of caufes
" which are far from being obvious, and
" which frequently efcape our obferva-
" tion. It would therefore be of great
" importance to philofophical fcrutiny, if
" the pofition of the mind, in any given
" circumftances, could be fixed till it was
" deliberately furveyed; if the caufes
" which alter its feelings and operations
" could be accurately fhewn, and their
" effects afcertained with precifion." To
accomplifh thefe ends, the dramatic writers, and particularly Shakefpeare, may be
of the greateft ufe. An attempt has accordingly been made, in the preceding
difcourfes, to employ the light which he
affords us in illuftrating fome curious and
interefting views of human nature.

In Macbeth, mifled by an overgrown
and gradually perverted paffion, " we
" trace the progrefs of that corruption,
" by which the virtues of the mind are
" made to contribute to the completion

8   " of

" of its depravity." In Hamlet we have a ftriking reprefentation of the pain, of the dejection, and contention of fpirit, produced in a perfon, not only of exqui-fite, but of moral and correct fenfibility, by the conviction of extreme enormity of conduct in thofe whom he loves, or wifhes to love and efteem. We obferve in Jacques, how

" Goodnefs wounds itfelf,
" And fweet affection proves the fpring of woe."

We fee in Imogen, that perfons of real mildnefs and gentlenefs of difpofition, fearing or fuffering evil, by the ingrati-tude or inconftancy of thofe on whofe affections they had reafon to depend, are more folicitous than jealous; exprefs re-gret rather than refentment; and are more apt to be overwhelmed with forrow than inflamed with revenge. In contem-plating the character of Richard the Third, we fee, and are enabled to explain, the ef-fect produced upon the mind by the difplay

of

of great intellectual ability, employed for inhuman and perfidious purpofes. We are led, on the other hand, by an obvious connection, to obferve, in the character of Falftaff, the effect produced on the mind by the difplay of confiderable ability, directed by fenfual appetites and mean defires. King Lear illuftrates, that mere fenfibility, uninfluenced by a fenfe of propriety, leads men to an extravagant expreffion both of focial and unfocial feelings; renders them capricioufly inconftant in their affections; variable, and of courfe irrefolute, in their conduct. In Timon of Athens, we have an excellent illuftration of felf-deceit, difplayed in the confequences of that inconfiderate profufion which affumes the appearance of liberality, and is fuppofed, even by the inconfiderate perfon himfelf, to proceed from a generous principle; but which, in reality, has its chief origin in the love of diftinction.

But

But while Shakefpeare furnifhes excellent illuftrations of many paffions and affections, and of many fingular combinations of paffion, affection, and ability, in various characters, we perceive, in the juftnefs of his imitation, the felicity of his invention. While he ' holds up a ' mirror,' in which we recognize the features and complexions of many powers and principles in the human mind, we muft admire that fine polifh by which they are received and reflected. He may be irregular in the ftructure of his fable, incorrect in his geographical or hiftorical knowledge, and too clofe an imitator of nature in his mixture of ferious and ludicrous incidents; for thefe are his principal errors: but in the faithful difplay of character, he has not hitherto been furpaffed. Nor can the carelefsnefs imputed to him in fome other refpects, be charged upon him, without injuftice, in his portraits of human life.

The

The true method of eftimating his merit in this particular, is by fuch an examination as in the preceding difcourfes has been fuggefted, and in fome meafure attempted. General remarks are often vague; and, to perfons of difcernment, afford fmall fatisfaction. But if we confider the fentiments and actions, attributed by the poet to his various characters, as fo many facts; if we obferve their agreement or difagreement, their aim, or their origin; and if we clafs them according to their common qualities, or connect them by their original principles, we fhall afcertain, with fome accuracy, the truth of the reprefentation. For, without having our judgments founded in this manner, they are liable to change, error, and inconfiftency. Thus the moralift becomes a critic : and the two fciences of ethics and criticifm appear to be intimately and very naturally connected. In truth, no one who is unacquainted

with

with the human mind, or entertains improper notions of human conduct, can
difcern excellence in the higher fpecies of
poetical compofition.

It may be faid however, in a fuperficial
or carelefs manner, ' that in matters of
this kind, laborious difquifition is un-
neceffary: and that we can perceive or
feel at once, whether delineations of
character be well or ill executed.'—Perfons, indeed, of fuch catholic and intuitive
tafte, require no erudition.   Confcious
of their high illumination, they will fcorn
refearch, and reject enquiry.   Yet many
of thofe who find amufement in fine writing, cannot boaft of fuch exquifite and
peculiar endowments.   As they need
fome inftruction before they can determine concerning the merit of thofe delineations that imitate external objects ;
fo they need no inconfiderable inftruction
before they will truft to their own impreffions concerning the difplay of the human
mind.

mind. Now, if criticifm be ufeful in forming, or in rectifying our tafte for what is excellent in language, imagery, and arrangement of parts, it is furely no lefs ufeful in regulating our judgment concerning the imitation of human powers and propenfities. Or is it an eafier matter to determine whether an affection of the mind be called forth on a fit occafion, exprefied with no unfuitable ardor, and combined with proper adjuncts ; than to judge concerning the aptnefs of a comparifon, or the fymmetry of a fentence ? Yet, in the prefent ftate of literary improvement, none, without being confcious of having cultivated their powers of tafte, will decide with affurance concerning the beauties either of imagery or of language : and none, whofe range of obfervation has been extenfive, will pronounce the knowledge of human nature, of the paffions and feelings of the heart, a matter of much eafier attainment. If

the

the difplay of character require the higheft exertion of poetical talents, that fpecies
of criticifm which leads us to judge concerning the poet's conduct in fo arduous
an enterprize, is not inferior, or unimportant.

Add to this, that the differences of
opinion concerning fome of Shakefpeare's
moft diftinguifhed characters, which the
author of thefe imperfect effays has had
occafion to remark, fince they were
firft offered to an indulgent public, are
fufficient to fatisfy him, that fuch dif-
quifitions may not only be amufing, but
have a direct tendency to eftablifh, on a
folid foundation, the principles of found
criticifm. Any thing further on this
fubject would be fuperfluous. Thofe
who have a true relifh for genuine and a-
greeable imitations of human nature, and
whofe judgments are not mifled by prejudice, even though they fhould receive
immediate enjoyment from the delinea-

tions

tions they contemplate, and be inftanta-neoufly inclined to pronounce them juft; will receive additional fatisfaction, if, by the difpaffionate award of reafon, their feelings are juftified, and their prepoffeffions confirmed.

F I N I S.

www.ingramcontent.com/pod-product-compliance
Lightning Source LLC
Chambersburg PA
CBHW060616030726
47498CB00005B/1692